Murder Well Done

An Old School Cozy Diner Mystery

by
Constance Barker

Chapter One

I refilled my coffee cup behind the counter of my little café, The Old School Diner, for the third time this morning.

"What's the matter? You don't like the way I pour your coffee any more, Mercy?" Deloris said in her faux-grumpy style as she handed me two packets of liquid creamer. "Now, scat. This is my counter; you don't belong back here." She pulled a compact mirror out of her trademark blonde beehive hairdo and put a wayward strand of hair back in place beneath a bobby pin. "I've been minding this counter since you were in diapers, and all of a sudden my coffee pouring isn't good enough for you?"

I smiled and sat at the end of the counter. "It's not that, Deloris. I just need to *do* something.

Sometimes I feel useless around here." I put my chin on my hand and leaned glumly on the counter.

"That's how it's supposed to be, Merse. You're the queen, and we're the worker bees." Deloris set down two plates of pancakes and eggs on the counter, and Babs delivered them to the Gallagher brothers.

Gilbert and Dickie Gallagher were aging twins who used to run the D&G Realty House until they retired a year ago and sold it to Joan Pianowski. She was the mayor's tough-as-nails assistant for many years, but now she's Paint Creek's newest council member – with ambitions to replace Mayor Finster, if he ever decides to retire.

"Why do you have that arm in a sling, Gilbert? Broken bone?" Babs asked as walked up to their table.

"Oh, no, nothing like that. Uh…my bursitis is acting up, and it hurts when I move it."

"Well, you take care of it, and get better soon, Gilbert!" She set the steaming platters in front of them, as well as the syrup decanter, which she had hooked on her little finger.

"Nice pancakes, Babs!" Gilbert said with his constant smile.

"Perfectly golden brown…" Dickie added, with a nod.

"…and the syrup is warm, the way we like it too!"

"Yeah!"

I always got a kick out of these two, the way they finished each other's sentences and were always so nice and bubbly. The duo reminded me of George and Lennie from *Of Mice and Men*. Like George, Gilbert was intelligent, though uneducated. And like Lennie, Dickie was a big man with strong hands, though a bit low on the brain power, it seemed. Red liked to say that Dickie was a few steps short of a Tango, but both brothers are Paint Creek treasures.

"I always take care of my boys!" Babs said as she bounced back to the counter and gave me a concerned look. "Why so down-in-the-dumps, Mercy?" The round 50-ish waitress handled all the tables and booths while Deloris took care of the counter, the beverage stations, and the pass-through window from the kitchen. Watching these two women run the dining room was like watching a well-choreographed ballet.

"Oh, I'm not really down, Babs. Just…bored, I guess."

I had been an ER nurse in Louisville for

several years and came back to my hometown of Paint Creek, Kentucky two years ago to buy the diner that my grandfather had opened over 50 years ago. I really love it here, but the pace is just so much slower.

"Sometimes I guess I miss the action of the big city. Maybe that's why I feel bored and out-of-sorts lately. I just wish I had a little more excitement in my life."

"Bored! My goodness, Mercy, there's never a dull moment here in Paint Creek. Why, just last week I went to pick up my nephew – you know Geronimo Jr. – from soccer practice at Paley Park out by the new church. Well, before I knew it, five of his teammates had piled into my little car! Hehe! If that's not excitement, I don't know what is!"

"Scintillating story, Babsy," Deloris snarked as she slid her a full pot of fresh coffee for refills. "If I ever need somebody to talk me down off a ledge, tell them not to send you."

"Well, just dig deep and look to the little things for fun and fulfillment, Mercy," she said as she bounced off to do a round of refills.

Maybe she had a point, but I still couldn't shake this funk I had fallen into.

"Hidee ho there, boys and girls!" Old Red

came in pulling his oxygen tank behind him on a little two-wheeler. "Hey, there, Gilbert. What'd I miss at Whittling Club last night? I decided to go to the town council meeting instead."

Deloris filled the special big red coffee mug she always used for Red and butted casually into his conversation. "I thought council meetings were on Thursday nights, Red."

"Yeah, well, Bud and his wife signed up for ballroom dancing on Thursdays, so they moved the meetings to Tuesdays for now. He's the Mayor, so, you know…he makes the rules. Maybe we should change whittling to Thursdays."

Dickie smiled broadly and pulled a freshly carved hummingbird out of his shirt pocket. "This is what I whittled last night."

"And I'll paint it later on this week," Gilbert said.

"Looks like some pretty good work there, Dickie. Hardwood, huh? I'm still trying to get the hang of whittling a bar of soap and balsa wood."

"Bring your pocket knife by the house, Red, and I'll sharpen it for you," Dickie offered. "That'll probably help a lot."

"Well, thank you, Dickie. I'll do that." Red looked around before he sat down at his customary spot in the middle of the counter. "Where's my fan club?" he asked, referring to Jake Carter and Junior, who were some of our other daytime regulars.

"You're ten minutes early, Red. They'll be coming along shortly. *Smoke!*" Deloris hollered to our aptly-named cook through the pass-through, "One pancake and a one-egg country scramble. Henry's here." Smoke always called Red by his real name.

She was waiting for his usual "Yes, ma'am," but Smoke didn't respond. She looked through the food window.

"What in the world…?"

Two seconds later, huge billows of grey, foul-smelling smoke came rolling through the pass-through window and swinging doors.

Babs and I turned to each other with the same *what-in-the-world* look that Deloris still had on her face. This was not the typical kind of smoke we were used to from Smoke's little grill fires. The 66-year-old cook came rushing out of the kitchen with a fire extinguisher in one hand. He didn't say a word, but just motioned for us to follow him. Several of us followed him through the kitchen and out the back door. I flipped on the big vent fan in the hood over the grill and stove, setting it to "high" on the way by, to get rid of most of the smoke. I closed the back door behind me, and we all stared at the dumpster, which was smoking profusely. The fire in the dumpster was out, but Smoke gave it another shot with the extinguisher as billows of residual smoke continued to rise from it.

"You brought us all out here to see a dumpster fire that you already put out, Smoke?" Red asked, making sure to keep his oxygen far from the heat.

The garbage truck was just coming up the alley and turning toward the dumpster to empty it, but Smoke waved him by and then turned to Red.

"No, Henry," Smoke shook his head. "It's not the fire I brought you out here to see."

Deloris covered her nose with a lacey handkerchief she pulled from her beehive and stepped up to the dumpster. I was a step behind her and looked in at a charred mess, but there was still too much smoke to see it well.

"Yup," Deloris said, "I guess you brought us out here to see a pile of ashes."

"You'd better not get too close, Deloris," I suggested. "Your hairspray might be flammable."

"It's just the propellant that's flammable," she said, "so I never use the aerosol kind. I work in a restaurant, Mercy. I wouldn't be crazy enough to use hairspray that's going to catch on fire – especially not with that accidental arsonist, Smoke Kowalski, slinging hash a few feet away from me." She turned away and wrinkled her nose. "It smells like Liz's salon around that dumpster," she said holding her nose with the hanky. Then she turned to Smoke, who was still agitated. "Is there something in there you want us to see, Smoke?"

Smoke grabbed a large piece of cardboard from the recycling bin nearby. "Wait." He fanned it briskly over the dumpster to clear the smoke away.

Gradually, we were able to make out a form, depressed in the middle of the partially burned trash. More people were gathered around the dumpster now, and Babs and I looked at each other.

"It's a…body," she said with wide eyes.

"Yup, a dead guy," Deloris said, matter-of-factly. "I'm going back to work." I swear, nothing dazed that woman.

Red had taken off his oxygen tubes and hung them over the tank on his hand cart. He filled the water bucket that Smoke used to clean the little tarred area out back and dumped it on the head of the corpse. Most of the fire had been on the other side of the dumpster where the corpse's legs were, and it seemed that Smoke had put it out pretty quickly after it started. The water washed away some of the loose ash, and Red sighed.

"That's Tommy Hopkins," he said, rubbing his chin, "Harold and Chrissy's boy. He's about your age, isn't he, Mercy? 33, 34?"

I was stunned, but I nodded. He was a class ahead of me, and probably the best-liked person in school – and in the town. He was captain of the basketball team the year we went to state, and half the girls in school had a crush on him. I was more into the debate squad and trumpet players, but he was a really great guy. *How could he end up like this?* He was even elected to the Town Council right after I moved back to town. I handed out pamphlets for his campaign at the county fair.

"Call Stan," I told Babs, and I texted Sheriff Brody Hayes. The Sheriff is kind of my boyfriend, although I haven't seen much of him lately. His main office is in Calhoun, seven miles away, and his deputy, Stan Doggerty, is in charge of law enforcement for Paint Creek.

I had just hit "send" when I heard a single *whoop* from Stan's patrol car as he rolled up the alley and stopped by the dumpster with his red and blue lights flashing.

"Been getting a lot of complaints," Stan said looking directly at me as he stepped out of his vehicle. "It's illegal to burn rubbish in your dumpster, Miss Howard. I'm going to have to write you up." He took his pad of tickets out of his back pocket and pulled a pen from the band of his cap.

"Oh, Stan!" Babs took him by the arm and walked him up to the dumpster. "We're not burning garbage, you silly goose. Look!"

Stan did a double take when he saw the dead body. "I'm pretty sure this is illegal too! I better get the Sheriff here."

"He's on his way, Stan," I said as I read the incoming text from Brody on my phone. "Why don't you tape off the area, and the rest of us will go back inside and have some coffee. Babs, maybe you can bring Stan a nice cold lemonade."

Chapter Two

The whole diner was abuzz with talk and speculation about the murder.

"He didn't have a butler, so it's got to be the wife," Pete Jenkins, a local farmer, declared.

"Oh, don't be silly, Pete," countered Tilly Meddler. "Patty is barely five feet tall and 95 pounds soaking wet. How is she going to get a big man like that into a dumpster? Besides, they were so happy, and their life together was really starting to take off. Their second baby is due in September, and they just built a new house on the hill on the east side."

I chuckled to myself, because the east side of Paint Creek is about a three-minute drive from the west side. I lived on the hill there too. But she did make some good points about Patty.

Jake and his son, Junior, pulled up right in front in Jake's big red pick-up truck. They ran the local construction and company, Carter & Son. This should be interesting, as these two always have a take on things that is, shall we say…unique.

Jake went right to the counter and sat by Red, while Junior paused to take a deep breath of the air that still had lingering odors from the blast of smoke.

"Mmmm! Smells good!" Junior said, as everyone turned to give him a strange look. "Is Smoke having a pig roast today? The meat smells pretty good, but..." he sniffed twice, "...I think the wood he's using is still a little green. Smells a little off."

Red and Jake were best of friends, but Red always had a bad comment about Junior's intellect, much to his dad's chagrin.

"There's no pig roast, you imbecile." Red rolled his eyes and shook his head.

"That was uncalled for, Red," Jake said in defense of his son as Junior took the stool next to him. "You're always picking on my boy."

"You're boy is 25-years old, Jake. He can defend himself. I don't mean to be picking on him, but the meat he's smelling, and getting all hungry over, is a dead body in the dumpster out back. Tom Hopkins was killed and tossed in the dumpster, and then the killer set it on fire."

"Holy smoke!" Jake burst out, a little too loudly.

"Somebody call my name?" Smoke asked from the kitchen.

"Nope," Delores answered him. "Just the regular rowdy crowd talking too loud."

"Oh…you be nice to my Jakey," Babs said to Deloris, giving him a kiss on the cheek and then tapping his nose with her finger as she whizzed by with a tray of dirty dishes.

"I don't know what you see in that smelly old fart anyway, Babsy. He's five years younger than you – and he never pays any attention to you anyway." Deloris just shook her head as she flipped the switch to grind the beans for a fresh pot of coffee.

"A girl can dream!"

"One girl's dream is another girl's nightmare, Babsy."

Red chuckled and slapped Jake on the back, but his buddy seemed totally unaware that the girls were talking about him. Then he turned the conversation back to the dead body out back. "It looks like your space aliens are at it again, Jake. They probably took poor Tommy up into their flying saucer and accidentally burned him up with one of their laser beams when they dropped him into the dumpster."

That did sound like one of Jake's conspiracy theories, but Junior is never one to be outdone.

"It could be spontaneous combustion, Pops. We'd better go out and take a look so we can figure out what really happened."

"I think you got it solved there, Junior," Red chided. "He was probably just sitting out there in the dumpster, minding his own business, and burst into flames. Stan's got it taped off out there, Junior, and Sheriff Hayes is probably there waiting for the CSI team by now too, so you might not see much right now."

Jake and Junior got up. "Maybe so, but we better check it out, Red. These detectives today never get it right, so me and Junior will probably have to solve it for them, as usual. Come on, Junior. Can we go through the kitchen, Mercy?"

"Be my guest."

"Hey, Pops," Junior said to Jake as they rounded the counter, "I wonder if it was those little mischief genies we've been seeing on the streets at night…"

Mischief genies?

"…You know how they always find an evil way to grant wishes – well, maybe somebody wished for some excitement or something, so they gave them a dumpster fire with a dead guy in it."

Great…now this terrible murder is my fault!

"Hey, Mercy," Deloris hollered, "this soda pop dispensing system is acting up again. Sully did a few things to it when he cleaned the lines last week, but it's still leaking all over the place, it doesn't keep the beverages cold, and it's impossible to set the syrup mixture right. I have to fiddle with it every day, but people are still complaining."

"I'll look into it, Deloris." I have looked into it, and a new machine is just too expensive.

"And that ice machine in the kitchen takes forever to make a batch of ice. Then I gotta drag a heavy bucket of ice all the way over to this rusty bin here."

Several heads turned to look at me. "It's not rusty, Deloris. It's just…old."

"Old, and full of holes in the old sheet metal."

She set down a color brochure in front of me. It was a beautiful new restaurant soda machine with a built-in icemaker on top. It filled up the bin automatically and dispensed the ice into the glasses.

"It'll fit perfectly on the back bar, and I won't have to carry a five-gallon bucket of ice or bend over to scoop it into the glasses."

"It's beautiful, Deloris – but it's almost two-thousand dollars. I just can't…"

She slapped a business card on the counter in front of me. "Lease to own. You'll save on water, maintenance, and refrigeration costs if you upgrade, Mercy. Isn't my health and happy customers worth four-and-a-half dollars a day for 16 months?"

I sighed. I knew I was defeated and picked up the card. "I'll call…Mr. Troy Stargill, Deloris."

"No need. I called him yesterday. He'll be here at 10:30 tomorrow morning, when it's slow, to talk to you about it."

"Four-fifty a day, Deloris?"

She nodded. "$135 a month for 16 months."

"Fine. Have him bring the machine with him and set it up tomorrow."

Chapter Three

Most of the hubbub over Tom Hopkins died down by the end of the lunch rush, and the diner was almost empty now. I was back at the end of the counter, with my chin in both hands this time, sipping on an orange soda.

"I can't believe that Brody was out back for nearly an hour this morning and didn't even come in to say hello to me, Deloris."

She put an empty cup in front of me and went back to rolling silverware.

I looked at her like a confused puppy. "What's this?"

"It's a cup of self-pity – and it doesn't look very good on you, Mercy."

"But…geez, Deloris, he's supposed to be my guy, and…"

She set an empty glass in front of me this time.

"Let me guess," I said. "A glass of whine."

"Mercy Howard, two months ago you were a powerful, self-sufficient woman who didn't need a man and could handle anything the world threw at you. And today, you're a high school pom pom girl sitting by the phone hoping that Johnny is going to ask you to the Prom."

"But…"

"But nothing. That man is the Sheriff of all of McLean County. He had a dead body and a team of crime scene investigators out there to manage, not to mention reporters and a half-dozen deputies looking for a plan to follow. And two more dumpster fires were called in while he was here too. So, boo hoo hoo."

"I thought you didn't like Brody – you thought he was hiding something."

"I changed my mind – when you told me he was in Afghanistan. That's what I was seeing. I saw a lot of my friends come back from Vietnam, and it changed them. War can play with a man's head, Mercy. Now it's you I'm worried about. Brody just needs someone to help him heal his emotional scars. Now, I could use some help filling this ice bin if you really want to make yourself useful."

"Okay, Deloris. You're right." I got up and grabbed the big white bucket under the counter. "And you know, this orange soda really does taste like…"

"Panther piss? That's what I've been telling you."

Deloris had a way with words. My phone vibrated loudly on the counter, and I looked at the text that was coming in. It was from Brody:

Sorry I didn't have time to come in and squeeze you, babe. Really busy lately, busier now. I'm going to need my Watson to help me out with this new case – another crazy one! Meet me for a quick bite later? I love you...Brody

I responded:

Sounds good, Brody! Paley Park 6:30, I'll bring sandwiches. <3 Mercy

Okay, I'm good now. I guess I just needed some reassurance. Deloris caught the big smile on my face as I put down my phone.

"Looks like Johnny called." She raised one eyebrow and grinned slyly.

I stuck out my tongue at her.

"Real mature, Merse."

Fortunately, Jake and Junior came through the door for their afternoon snack, and we both focused our attention back on business.

"Here come the Hobbits for their second breakfast," she said softly to me.

They were both short and looked a lot like

overweight Hobbits. "Good afternoon, guys," I greeted them. They nodded and sat down at the counter with serious looks on their faces.

"Don't you two have a home?" Deloris said as she set down a glass of water for each of them.

I shot her the evil eye, and she plastered on a phony smile.

"Zack is cooking this afternoon, guys. He needs some guinea pigs to try his Salisbury steak special, if you're interested. Smoke's out, so there's no turkey." Zack was the high school kid that Smoke had taken on as his apprentice.

"Sounds good to me," Jake said.

Junior shook his head. "Not for me, Deloris. I just want a little snack. Give me a couple of those half-pound bacon cheeseburgers, a slice of apple pie, and a double chocolate malted milk."

"I thought you were starting on a diet today, Junior," his dad reminded him.

"Oh, yeah. You better add a Chef's Salad with extra French dressing and a scoop of mayonnaise on top too. Medium-well on the burgers, please."

"Anything else there, Junior? Maybe a couple of horses and a herd of piggies?"

"Deloris…" I said disapprovingly through my

teeth.

"Nope, just that…and a big basket of French fries, of course. And a scoop of ice cream on the pie."

"Sure thing, boys. Smoke has a fresh keg of beer in his refrigerator. Would you…?"

Jake waved her off. "Nope, no beer for us today, Deloris. We've got a murder to solve."

Oh, boy. Jake and Junior are going to try to crack this murder case. Well, maybe they'll stumble across something.

"Have you found out anything yet, Jake? Any clues?" I asked.

"Well, it looks like Tom was the only member of the city council who was against the mayor's plan to put in new streets with curbs and gutters in the old part of town where Bud lives, and he was trying to win over some of the other council members to vote No too."

"Interesting, but is that really a motive for murder? Half the town lives there. The residents there are all in favor of it." Bud Finster had been the mayor of Paint Creek forever, and upgrading those old streets had been talked about for years. Maybe they were finally getting around to it.

"A lot of big contracts, not to mention property values, are riding on this vote, Mercy. Junior and I just put in a new kitchen for Bud last year, and property values there are just not going up, so it doesn't pay to renovate anymore. Everybody wants to move to the hill over Northeast, where you live, Mercy. This street upgrade would probably add 20 percent to property values in the south neighborhood, and revitalize the area. Some people are getting notices that their property value has been cut in half because of the poor streets. Bud has a few empty lots there too that he can't unload, but for sure they would be in high demand if the neighborhood streets are fixed up."

"I guess…but revitalization sounds like a good thing for Paint Creek." I wondered why Tom would be opposed to the plan. He ran a small accounting firm from an office at Builders' Trust and Savings downtown, and a few years ago he took a job as the head loan officer at the bank too. It's a small town, so it wasn't a problem to do both jobs from one office. "Why was Tom opposed to the revitalization measure? I mean, as a loan officer shouldn't he want property values to go up? He would make higher commissions on bigger loans."

"Tom said we needed the money to improve the high school and build a new elementary, not line the pockets of politicians – says we should put the project off for one year. Red was at the council meeting, and that's what he told me."

Tom must have really been sincere in his opposition to the plan. I could see the wheels turning in Jake's head as he guzzled his entire glass of water and set it on the counter very indelicately. Maybe he was doing some good work on this case after all.

"Follow the money." Junior blew the paper wrapper off his straw and poked it into his malted milk.

Okay, I'll bite. "What money, Junior?"

"Well, Tom Hopkins was a banker and an accountant, right? Streets and schools and things – they cost a lot of money." He leaned towards Jake and me and spoke a little more softly. "I can't prove it yet, but I'm pretty sure he had a printing press in the basement of the Village Hall. He figured, since he's the one printing up all the money, he should get to be the one to decide how to use it. He was just starting to raise his kids, so he wanted the money to go for schools. And it's a little fishy that he had money to build a new house over Northeast. I heard he paid cash for it. He's moving out of the old side of town, so he didn't want his money to be spent there, ya see?" He nodded his head once and winked at me, as if to emphasize the huge importance of his wisdom.

It always boggles my mind how Junior can mix absurd ideas together with things that make so much sense. "That's fascinating, Junior. You should consider a career in law enforcement."

"No can do, Mercy. Doesn't pay enough, and I'd have to go to work every day, wash my uniform…nah. I'll stick with construction. A couple good contracts a month, and that's all it takes."

Thank God for small favors. I filled the ice bin – that big bucket was heavy! – and headed for home to relax and get ready for my picnic dinner with Brody.

Chapter Four

"Hi, Gracie! Did you miss me? Oh, it looks like you and Wizard really like my homemade kibble…it's all gone!"

My little hamsters were my best friends when I was at home, and, yes, I talked to them all the time.

"Wizzy, is Grace letting you get enough to eat? She's getting a little pudgy. Or is she just not as active as you?" I took Wizard out of the cage and petted his luxurious fur with my finger. "You're my favorite, you know," I whispered softly into his ear so Gracie couldn't hear me. "Okay, back you go. I have to jump into the shower now. I'll feed you before I go."

I had plenty of time, so I washed my hair to make sure that I wouldn't smell like dumpster smoke when I met Brody. I toweled off my body, went into my room, and held my towel open behind me in front of my full-length mirror on the door.

"Almost bikini-ready," I said to myself as I poked my finger in and out of the little bit of fat just below my belly button. "Better than last week." I looked briefly at the bathroom scale on the floor and decided I wasn't brave enough to step on it today. "But I guess there will be more early morning jogs for me for another week or so."

I started to dry my hair. "Cross your fingers, Mercy." I never knew if it would be a good or bad hair day until my hair was dry. It was a humid day, so my natural waves were a little more pronounced in my long blonde tresses. "Not bad." I squinted at the mirror, tilted my head, and scrunched my mouth to one side, which is my decision-making face.

"So…ponytail or down? *Wizard!*" I hollered out of my bedroom door, "How should I wear my hair? Ponytail? Okay, thanks, that's what I was thinking too." He was always helpful with these kinds of decisions – and Brody always likes it when I unleash my locks and shake them loose. Plus, the ponytail works well with my white visor cap.

It was a warm July day, so I put on some bright yellow shorts and a lime green tank top over my favorite push-up bra and walked past my little buddies and into the kitchen. It was just separated from the living room by my granite-top peninsula and breakfast nook.

"Well, thank you, Wizard, but I think 'smoking hot' might be a bit of an exaggeration." He was always very generous with his compliments, and yes, I'm a little crazy when I'm at home. I just don't like being alone, so my hamsters are more like roommates that I chat with. Don't judge me!

I put on a pot of coffee and tried to get some ideas for my casual dinner with Brody. "Time to put together a nice picnic dinner for Brody and me…let's see what we have in the refrigerator. What's that? No, Gracie. If I have Zack or Smoke make something for me it won't be, you know…personal." Her ideas were never as good as Wizard's.

The doorbell rang, which almost never happened. *I wonder who that is?* I opened the door, expecting a sales pitch for Girl Scout cookies or an opportunity to have the greenest lawn on the block for the price of a cup of coffee a day. Instead, I was surprised to see a beautiful, classy young woman with golden cappuccino skin, hypnotic hazel eyes, and a plate of cookies in her hand.

My jaw dropped and I forgot how to speak. "Uh… hi! Um…"

She smiled, flashing her flawless white teeth and laughed as she spoke. "Hi, I'm Ruby Owana, your new neighbor."

Wow! A neighbor and potential friend I might be able to relate to. "Come in! Come in, Ruby." I enthusiastically pulled the door all the way open. "I'm Mercy Howard."

"I know." Ruby put one foot tentatively across the threshold and peered from side to side. "Is this a good time? I thought I heard you talking to somebody."

I turned a little red and motioned my hand toward the hamster cage. "Just working out the finer points of my life with my little friends, Grace and Wizard."

Ruby chuckled and handed me the plate of cookies. "We're the same…I talk to my little pooch all the time. Oh, look!" she said enthusiastically as she ventured inside. "The little one has a lightning bolt on his forehead! You must be Wizard."

I was pleasantly flabbergasted. "Oh, my goodness, Ruby! Everyone else laughs at me when I tell them that dark splotch of fur is a lightning bolt. You're the first one to see that he looks exactly like Harry Potter."

"The spitting image – of the young Harry in the first episode, that is."

"Of course!" I smiled. "I'm beginning to think I've found my soul sister."

"I hope so! Otherwise I'll be here all alone in

the big city…of Paint Creek."

We had the same sense of humor too. "Come in the kitchen. I have to put together a late lunch for my boyfriend and me." It felt good to say that. "The coffee should be ready. Now here's the big question that will determine if we're really compatible members of the cosmic sisterhood: How do you take your coffee?"

She got a make-believe worried look on her face. "If I get it wrong, am I out?"

I nodded. "Right out the door," I said with a wink.

"Well…two sugars, no cream is what I prefer, Mercy…but I can be flexible!"

"Perfect!" I said with a laugh.

"That's how you like your coffee too?"

"Nope. Two creams, no sugar for me. So, we will complement one another perfectly!" I poured her a cup of fresh hot coffee, pushed the sugar bowl her way, and put the cookies on the breakfast nook where she was sitting. "I should be the one bringing you a nice plate of goodies to welcome you to Paint Creek, Ruby. You shouldn't have brought these for me…and it looks like you've never eaten a cookie in your life."

She took a big bite out of one and answered, with her fingers in front of her full lush lips, as she was still chewing, "Oh, yes, I have!"

I took a bite too. "This is amazing!" It really was. "Banana…molasses…chocolate chip?"

Ruby nodded. "And macadamia nuts. Just a little banana to keep them from getting brittle."

I had never tasted a cookie like this before. "Yum! I'm going to pack one for Brody too."

"They're called *Sweet Mercy* cookies, because that's what you say when you take a bite."

"Ha! I like them even better now."

"It's my Grandma Ramona's recipe, Mercy. Actually, it's been in the family for generations, but I had to get it from my sister because Gran won't give out the recipe until we're married."

We fell into a conversation as if we had known each other forever. We talked about everything from the bar scene in Louisville, to our plans for the future, to our love life nightmares.

"But I think I might have gotten lucky this time," I said as I made a big meaty sandwich for Brody and a chicken salad wrap for myself. "Brody's kind of…one in a million."

"Brody is a lucky man," she said.

"True!"

She told me she was going to be the new history teacher at the high school, replacing my old teacher, Marla Dommish, who finally retired in June. Ruby was 28 now, five years younger than me, and had taught for a few years in the city. But she wanted to get some small-town experience. She thought the kids would be easier to handle and she could get into administration more quickly.

We talked and laughed for nearly an hour and got along like we had known each other all our lives. I found out that her mother was black and Native American and her father was Italian and Filipino, which explained her amazing exotic good looks, and maybe her Hawaiian-sounding last name too. She was smart, funny, and had a really kind heart. I hoped she would stay forever.

Eventually the conversation turned to the murder of Tom Hopkins. The news had already spread throughout the town.

"It's terrible," she said, shaking her head. "I met him and Patty when I was looking at houses. They were really excited about the new home they were building not far from here, and we talked in the yard there for quite a while. A lovely couple. I just can't believe it…and it's scary to think that there's a murderer running loose in this small town."

"Brody is a great investigator, Ruby," I reassured her. "The killer won't be on the loose for long."

"You seem to be handling this all in stride, Mercy."

"Well, that's what five years in the ER does to you. You learn to compartmentalize the inner torment, and then just have a day once in a while where you're in tears and wonder what kind of world we live in."

"I just came from the grocery store, and I heard there was another dumpster fire after the three this morning, Mercy."

"Really?" *My Gosh, that's four in one day. What's going on in Paint Creek?*

She nodded. "Thank goodness there haven't been any more dead bodies in any of them. You know, when I was a girl outside of Louisville, there was a rash of windshields being shot out of cars over night for a while." She gave a wry smile. "Turned out it was the local windshield glass replacement guy drumming up business for himself. Sorry…this rash of fires just made me think of that."

It was time for me to get going to meet Brody

now. "Ruby," I said to her seriously as she was getting up to leave, "I have an odd question for you…"

"Mmm okay. What, Mercy?"

"Will you be my best friend?"

She laughed and hugged me, and we both got a little misty-eyed. "You are just what I need in my life, Mercy. In fact, the reason I chose the house next door instead of the one on Earl Street is because the Realtor told me that the nice young woman who ran the diner lived here. You were a big selling point in my decision! I just never expected you would turn out to be a brilliant nurse, a real sweetheart, and the girlfriend of the County Sheriff. I feel like I hit the jackpot."

I held up my cup of coffee, still admiring her perfect golden skin, and made a toast. "Here's to my new best friend, the Golden Goddess of Paint Creek!"

She picked up her nearly empty cup and clinked with me. "And here's to my best friend, the Ivory Princess of McLean County!"

Chapter Five

Brody sneaked up behind the secluded park bench I was sitting on, finishing up a crossword puzzle on my phone while I was waiting. He was 15 minutes early, and startled me with a kiss on the cheek.

"Brody! Hi, hon. I was just going to text you to tell you where I was. How did you know where to find me? It's a big park."

"Well, lovely lady," he said with sly smile as he came around the bench with a handful of dandelions and pulled me up by the hand, "I know my girl pretty well. This is about the only bench in the park that's out of sight from prying eyes along the road and around the ball fields and swings." He hugged me around the waist, and I nuzzled my face into his chest. "And I'm pretty sure you didn't come here for the sandwiches."

He was right about that. I took off my cap and put one of the dandelions in my hair. We kissed for several seconds, long enough to feel the tingles, until Brody cut it off.

We sat, and I handed him half of the roast beef sandwich, from which he took a ravenous bite immediately.

"So, what's happening with this crazy case, Brody? Any leads or theories yet?"

"Well, we have a few different paths to check out. We have to check out the wife, of course, and then there are all of the business clients from his accounting business and all those financial trails."

"I see. Lots to do. But I think he was spending most of his time doing home loans and second mortgages recently." I dangled my feet from the park bench and kicked at a dandelion in the grass as I filled my lungs with the sweet country air from the gentle summer breeze. "So, how was Tom killed?"

Brody shrugged "I didn't see any bullet holes, but I don't like to get too close to dead bodies. I leave that to the medical people. We're still waiting for the autopsy, but Sylvia will be doing it at eight o'clock tonight."

"Really? Does she need any help?"

"I can get you in there if you want. She was impressed with your observations on the case we had a while back, so I'm sure she would appreciate having a trauma nurse around to bounce ideas off of."

"Great. I'll be there. So, what about the town council connection?"

"What connection is that? I know he was a council member, but how is that relevant?"

"Well, you know…he was the only one opposed to putting in the new streets with curb and gutter on the south side of town. Property owners there, plus some big contractors, stand to gain a lot if the council passes the upgrade."

"Interesting, Mercy," Brody said as he finished up the last bite of his sandwich and reached for one of the cookies Ruby had brought me. "Good work, coming up with that. I didn't know."

"Well, actually, it was Jake who came up with that information."

"Jake Carter? *Your* Jake from the diner?"

"Well, I wouldn't call him *my* Jake, but yup. That's the one"

"I can't believe that Jake and Junior actually came up with some helpful information."

"Hey, I didn't say anything about Junior. He's pretty sure that Tom was killed because he was printing money from his printing press in the basement of the Village Hall. There's a little more to his idea than that, but I'll spare you the details."

"Mmm…good cookie. Yeah, that sounds more like Junior. But I'm down in that basement pretty often – it's where the evidence room for Paint Creek is, and we have a small armory down there – and Junior will be disappointed to learn that there's no printing press down there."

"Well, that doesn't prove anything, Brody. Tom's henchmen probably just beamed it up to the mothership whenever they weren't using it."

"You have all the answers, Mercy. You should be the Sheriff." He put his official "Smokey" hat on my head and kissed my cheek. "You know, you're going to have to bake those cookies more often, Mercy. They're just so good. One bite and it's obvious that they were baked by a brilliant, beautiful woman with a heart full of love for children and small animals. If I'd never met you before, I would have fallen in love with you after the first bite. I'd ask for your recipe, but, hey…the chef is my girlfriend!"

I'm going to have to drug Ruby and put her on a slow boat to China. "Well, it's an old family recipe…" *just not my family.* "So, what have you been so busy with lately? I hardly heard from you at all this past week."

"Everything. Cotter's Junction can't support a police department anymore, so I'm hiring and training a new deputy for them and a couple of new deputies for the county too, plus the state is coming in to inspect our records, our vehicles, and our arsenal, making sure that everything is up to date and in compliance. And now we have this murder and this rash of dumpster fires, and they're not just in Paint Creek. There's something very odd about this case, Mercy. I'm going to need your help – you know, some eyes and ears here in Paint Creek."

"Sure, just let me know what you need." I saluted and gave him back his hat. "I'm here to help!"

"I'll make a plan and talk to you about the details at the diner in the morning, Mercy."

"You know, I could use some help from you too, Brody. My lips are a little dry…"

He got the idea and kissed me.

"Hoo! Almost as good as that cookie!" he said with a wink.

"I think you like kissing me, Sheriff Hayes."

"It's a dirty job, but somebody's got to do it."

We shared a laugh, but then my warm enthusiasm for our beautiful moment started to be replaced with melancholy as my mind raced with questions and uncertainties. I remembered that it had been nearly a week with hardly a word from Brody. Things seemed so hot and cold sometimes. Maybe he compartmentalizes me and his feelings for me the way I compartmentalize my feelings about death and trauma.

I hugged his arm and put my head on his shoulder. "Brody…is our romance a dumpster fire?"

He gave me a confused and worried look when he saw that my mood had turned serious. "What do you mean, Mercy? Our romance is great."

"I mean…like…when we're together, the fire burns hot and the flames are all-consuming. But then maybe later on there'll be nothing left but ashes. Maybe we'll burn up all the chemistry that fuels our attraction, and then there won't be anything left to keep the fire burning and keep our hearts warm."

He gave me a strained smile and held my chin tenderly in his strong hand. "Mercy," he said putting his face close to mine, "I was a Boy Scout, and I know how to tend a fire. Every time I look at you, it's like putting another log on the fire. And every time I kiss you it fans the flames to new heights. We're not starting at the peak and burning out, honey. We have a real relationship, which means we're just beginning to build our fire, and it gets warmer every day. The flames we have now? Those are nothing compared to what we will have next year and the year after that."

That's how I felt too, but I still had another question to ask: "Brody…what if you met somebody prettier who made better cookies?"

I think he didn't know if I was kidding around or not, and neither did I, truthfully. But he answered sincerely. "Mercy, do you think I love you for your pretty face and your sandwiches? Love is a lot more than looks and cookies, honey. I know it's only been a short time, but you're a part of my soul…of me. Here…"

He reached into his pocket and pulled out a keychain that held a tarnished pair of brass dog tags from his time in the military. He took one off the chain and handed it to me. "I've always kept these with me as a reminder of where I've been, Mercy. But now you're the other half of me, so you should hold on to one of them. Maybe this will help you understand that I'm always with you."

Chapter Six

It was beginning to feel like this day was never going to end! It started out like any other, taking care of business around the diner, until that horrible dumpster fire and the discovery of Tom Hopkins' body sent everything into a tailspin. But, I found my new best friend and moved my relationship with Brody back into a good place. It's already been a pretty remarkable day.

And now here I was, at the county morgue. I was in the little ready-room just outside the morgue, putting on some clean scrubs, a lab coat, latex gloves, and a surgical mask. *Now I'm ready to assist Sylvia Chambers with the autopsy of my friend...I think.* Actually, I wasn't sure at all if I was ready for this. I mean, I worked with a lot of cadavers in nursing school, and I've had a lot of experience with serious injuries in the ER. But watching the Medical Examiner pull body organs out of a man I grew up with, examine them, weigh them, and throw them in a bucket might be a little unnerving.

I walked the few steps to the door of the morgue at the end of the hall on the second floor of the public health building. I was engulfed in an eerie silence as I stopped with my hand on the door's push plate. The blinds were closed on the other side of the glass door, indicating to me that Sylvia had probably already begun the autopsy. I pushed opened the door and then knocked gently.

"Come on in, Mercy! Just getting started here. I hope you don't mind, but I've already made the 'Y' incision and removed the rib cage. Come on in! Come in! I want to show you the marks on the neck before we look inside."

My nurse instincts began to kick in, and I walked over to the table, across from Sylvia. "Oh, my! Ligature marks – Tom was strangled, Sylvia!"

"Yes, he was, and for a good long while by the looks of it."

I opened his eyelid with my thumb. I held back a gasp as I beheld his glassy, blood red eyes, and I noticed some bruising below the eyes as well.

"A lot of subconjunctival hemorrhaging, as you can see," Sylvia said, "along with some involuntary urination." She looked at the lower half of the body, which was covered in a sheet. "The legs are charred pretty badly, but the rest of the body seems to be in good shape, once I cleaned up all the smoke and ash residue."

She pulled back the flap of skin from his chest to reveal the inside of the neck, and I could see at once that he was indeed killed by strangulation.

"The hyoid bone is broken," I said. "It must

have been someone fairly strong to do that, I suppose."

"Well, not necessarily." Sylvia leaned casually on the table with one hand and waggled her finger with the other. "It's… mmmm, *kind of* a delicate bone, but with the use of a ligature a seventh-grader could probably break it."

"So, that doesn't really narrow down our possible types of suspects, I guess. The neck looks bruised…a lot of burst capillaries…but I don't see any rope burn from whatever kind of cord they used."

"Good point. Maybe it was a silk scarf or something smooth like that."

"What's this mark over here?" I asked her, pointing to what appeared to be a cut on Tom's neck.

"Well, I thought it might just be a nick he got when he was thrown in the dumpster, but "

"But it looks like he was still alive when he was cut. I'm no expert, but it seems his blood was still flowing."

Sylvia walked over to an evidence bag that held his clothes. She pulled out his white shirt, and we examined the collar together.

"Yeah, it looked like the cut would have been right above the top of his collar, and you can see quite a bit of blood on the collar here, Mercy. He was alive."

"Is there any way to tell what was used to make the cut, Sylvia?"

She shook her head and shrugged. "Probably not. It's not a stab wound, just a small slash, so it would be hard to get an idea of the length and shape of the blade or whatever was used. But whatever it was, the clean cut shows that it was sharp as a razor, no pulling or tearing. And look at this." She held up the collar and held it towards me.

"What? The blood?"

"No, next to it here. There's some kind of dust or dirt on the top of the collar, right where the blood stops, and then another little line of blood."

There was a light tan smudge by the blood stain, maybe a powdery substance. "I see...like maybe the blade scraped against it and wiped off some residue that was on it, and some blood that got on the edge of the blade when it made the slash."

She nodded. "It's probably nothing – there are always a lot of red herrings in an autopsy – but I'll send a sample to the lab to see if they can identify it. I'll take a swab from the wound on the neck too. I already vacuumed his hair and clothing to see if we can get any carpet fibers. I think he was placed in the trunk of a car, so we might get lucky and find some fibers that will identify the kind of vehicle."

We walked back to the autopsy table, and Sylvia recorded some remarks into the microphone.

I noticed some blue lividity marks on the body's right side and arm. "He was kind of on his left side in the dumpster," I said, "so shouldn't these marks be on the left, Sylvia?"

"The body was moved, Mercy. He died last night, sometime around 10:00, and I'd guess he spent the night in the trunk of a car, kind of in a half fetal position, with his knees bent so he would fit in the trunk."

"That's the same position he was in when we found him in the dumpster."

"Right. He was probably still in full rigor this morning when the killer tossed him in the dumpster, and he ended up on his left side in there. He was on his right side over night when the blood settled on his right side," she said, pointing to the blue lividity marks.

"It looks like there are some marks on his right

side too, maybe impressions from a plastic floor mat in the trunk."

"I'll get some pictures."

I'd seen enough and didn't stick around for the examination of all the internal organs. I could always read the report if she found anything important. I kind of wanted to watch her sew him back together when she was done, but my queasiness and feelings for my dead friend outweighed my scientific curiosity.

Chapter Seven

"Brrrrr! It's cold in that little walk-in cooler, Smoke," I said to my cook as I came out of the cooler after preparing my vegetable order. "You keep it pretty neat and organized in there, and everything has the date on it. I guess that's why we always get top marks from the health inspector."

"Who cares about the health inspector?" Smoke said as he sliced a fresh pork belly slab into thick strips of bacon. "That's why our friends and neighbors never get sick from spoiled food coming out of my kitchen." Smoke wiped his face with one of the white kitchen towels and threw it in the laundry sack. "Anyway…you know, Mercy, if it weren't for that cooler I'd never make it through the summer around this place. It gets mighty hot in this little kitchen."

"Especially when you start a fire on the grill, Smoke." Zack, Smoke's young assistant, had a big smile on his face as he hung up his apron and cap.

"Run along now, sonny. We don't need any wise-acres around here. Now go get some rest – you've got to be back here for lunch in two hours." He had a serious look for Zack but then turned to me with a smile and a wink as Zack headed out the swinging doors with a wave. The back was still a crime scene, so he had to go out the front.

"Heh heh," Smoke chuckled, "that boy is getting to be a pretty good cook you know, Mercy."

"He's learning it all from you, Smoke."

He smiled and got a nostalgic look on his face. "And I learned it all from your granddad, Mercy. I was 16, just a year or two younger than Zack is now, when your gramps hired me the day he opened this place. Of course, I learned a lot of cooking on a battleship that shuttled our soldiers between the war in Vietnam and some relaxing R&R in the Philippines too. If it weren't for what your grandpa taught me about cooking, I would have been carrying a rifle in the jungle instead of a spatula in the galley of a ship."

"Mercy! Come on out here. You've got a visitor!" Deloris hollered to me through the pass-through window.

I wonder who that could be? I grabbed my clipboard and little laptop and went out to the dining room.

"Hi, Neighbor! I thought I'd stop in and watch you work while I still have some free time before school starts in the fall."

"Ruby! Well, this is my home-away-from-home. Not exactly the Oakroom in Louisville, but it's all mine!"

"I love it! So clean and homey and…old school! I can see why it pulled you away from the big city."

"Deloris, coffee for my friend, please – 2 sugars, no cream. And a cup for me too. Thanks!"

I looked down the counter as I went to lead Ruby to my little booth by the window. Red, Jake, and Junior all had their stools turned around, staring at Ruby with their jaws hanging down.

"Aren't you gonna introduce us to Miss America, Mercy?" Red finally said, breaking out of his trance.

Ruby was embarrassed but turned to face the guys.

"This is my neighbor, Ruby Owana. She's the new history teacher at the high school. This is Red, Jake, and Junior. Now, you guys can stop gawking and make her feel welcome here."

Red jabbed Jake with his elbow but kept looking straight ahead at Ruby. "The boys in her class aren't going to learn a darn thing," he said softly.

"Nice to meet you guys!" She smiled and waved at them, and then we sat in the booth. "I already met Deloris and Babs," she told me.

I heard some clunking behind the counter as we sat down and noticed that the old soda machine had been disconnected and was sitting on the front counter. The new one was still covered in plastic near the spot where it would be installed on the back bar. Delores seemed to be talking to the installer, who was lying on the floor, probably working with the water line.

"Getting a new soda machine, I see," Ruby said.

I checked off the fruits and vegetables I needed and clicked the *Send* button on my produce supplier's website. "Yeah. We really needed it."

"You better be careful or you're going to have to change the name of your diner!" We laughed and then she looked out the window, "Uh-oh! It looks like you might be in trouble with the law. Here comes a tall, handsome officer with a gun." Then she whispered to me as Brody walked in the door, "He's really cute!"

I whispered back, "He's *my* cute officer, Ruby, so don't get any ideas!"

Brody pulled up a chair and sat down. "Hi, Mercy. Hi, Ruby."

I did a double take. "You two know each other?"

Ruby nodded. "I had to stop by the Sheriff's office to finish up my background check for the school."

"Yeah, she had some pretty suspicious activity on her rap sheet."

"Very, funny, Sheriff. I had one outstanding parking ticket that I didn't even know I had. I parked in front of a restaurant downtown in Louisville, and…"

"…and she thought the guy standing by the curb was a valet…"

"…so, I parked…"

"…in a tow away zone…"

"…and gave him my keys. Apparently, I got a parking ticket before the guy stole my car. Well, they never found my car, and I didn't know anything about the ticket until it showed up on my background check, so they sent me to see the Sheriff."

"Haha! That is so funny, Ruby! So, I guess you helped her clean up her record, Brody?"

"Well, I corroborated that her car was reported stolen on the same day she got the unpaid ticket.

Then she wrote a check, and I rubber stamped her form from the school."

"Mmhm. And…um…what else did you guys talk about?" I had to ask. I mean, there must have been some flirting going on, right?

Ruby rolled her eyes. "We barely talked at all! Sheriff Hayes was too busy talking on his cell phone with some mystery woman, trying to get her to go to dinner at the Hideaway."

"And, did she agree to go with you, Brody?" I asked with a smile.

"No! She was too busy running her diner…I mean, her nail and hair salon. Liz was busy that night."

I punched him. Liz ran the salon on the east end of town. She was a couple years younger than Brody, and he didn't like her at all, mostly because of her constant gossiping. "That's not funny, Brody."

"Good morning, folks. I'm Troy Stargill. Your soda machine and icemaker is all set."

He was tall and dark with captivating deep-set brown eyes. He was still young, maybe 25 or 30, with a chiseled superhero chin and a sparkling white smile.

Ruby stood up and extended her hand. "It's very nice to meet you, Mr. Stargill." She smiled brightly, and I thought she was going to drool on her chin.

"Well, you must be Mercy Howard, I guess."

"Nope," I said. "That would be me." I took his clipboard and signed the papers. "That's Ruby. She's new in town and just anxious to meet new people."

She shot me a disapproving look and then moved her gaze back to Troy Stargill. "I…was just being polite," she said. "And I don't know many people my age around here." She sat.

What am I? A dinosaur?

"Well, we'll have to fix that, Ruby. I work all the small towns around here in my business, and I'd say the best place to get to know people is at *Bangers* in Ballers Ferry."

"Bangers?" Ruby looked a little concerned – or maybe excited. I couldn't tell for sure.

"Oh, it's not as wild as it sounds. Live music and four-dollar Margaritas."

That piqued her interest. "Strawberry?"

Troy nodded. "Strawberry Margaritas too, Ruby. I'm going there tonight. Would you care to join me?"

"Sounds like fun!"

Wow. Dating must be easy for this girl. One handshake and a dozen words, and she's got a date with Mr. Handsome.

"I get into Paint Creek every week or so," Troy told Ruby. "I own and manage the coin-operated laundry machines at the Coin-o-mat downtown and in the new apartments out by the bourbon distillery. As a matter of fact, I'll be in town tomorrow to talk to Julia at the coffee shop about a new cappuccino machine. Maybe we can have lunch, Ruby."

"Well, let's start with the club tonight, Troy, and see how it goes. But I'm free until school starts in September. I'm a teacher."

Troy looked satisfied with her response and then turned to me. "Say, Ms. Howard, ma'am…I overheard the gentlemen at the counter talking about a fire you had in your dumpster out back."

"Yeah, it was quite something."

"Well, I work with a lot of schools and big companies, and we carry a product that they use in janitorial rooms, which are susceptible to catching on fire because of all the oily rags and cleaners and solvents. It'll smother a fire in a small enclosed space, and I'm sure it would work in a dumpster too, ma'am."

"Well, I'm pretty sure this was a one-time thing, you know."

"Oh…I don't know. I've heard there's been quite a spate of them, so you never know. A box of three is just 20 bucks. Just stick one under the lid, and it'll extinguish a small fire before it can get too big."

"I'll take my chances. The arsonist will probably open the lid before he starts the fire anyway."

"I guess I hadn't thought of that. We also carry a full line of security cameras so you can keep an eye on your business, inside and outside. We could just add it on to the contract."

"I never thought I'd need anything like that in Paint Creek," I said, "but it would be great if we could just look at the tape and see who put the dead body in the dumpster and set it on fire."

Troy turned white as a sheet. "Body? There was a body in the dumpster?"

He looked like he was getting weak in the knees, and I thought he might fall down. I quickly pulled a chair over from the nearby table and had him sit. Ruby ran to his side.

"Are you all right, Troy?" she asked, putting her hand on his shoulder.

"Oh, yeah. I'm fine. I haven't had lunch yet, so I guess I just got a little light-headed all of a sudden."

"Babs, we need a cheeseburger over here, stat!" Brody and Ruby gave me an odd look.

We got Troy to sip on some water and he started looking better. "Well, think about that security system, ma'am. It'll help you sleep at night."

"So, how come you call Ruby by her name and you call me *ma'am,* Troy?"

He was a little taken aback by my question, and stammered through his response. "Well, 'cause, um…she's…you know…um…a girl…ma'am."

Hmmphh! Glad I asked.

Chapter Eight

"I thought you boys had a construction job this afternoon," Deloris said to Jake and Junior, who were still sitting at the counter.

"Yeah, we do, but the supplies won't be ready

for us for another couple hours or so. I just checked with the lumber yard," Jake replied.

It was mid-afternoon. Red, Troy, and Ruby had just left after a nice lunch, and Brody and I joined Junior and Jake at the counter. Pete Jenkins came in and took a booth by the window.

"Well, this has been a pretty long lunch for me, Mercy, and I have to get back to work." Brody took a sip of his raspberry iced tea – a new flavor we were able to add with the new machine. "Good stuff. I might have to come around more often now that you have my favorite beverage…"

Your favorite girl isn't enough?

"…Anyway, I told you I was coming in today to tell you how you could help me out with this investigation."

All heads turned toward Brody when he brought up the murder investigation.

"Okay, folks…you're all deputized and sworn to secrecy. If you leak any of this classified information, I'll throw you in the hoosegow overnight – and I'm not kidding. Okay?"

Everyone nodded, and Pete joined us at the counter. Brody walked behind the counter, and Deloris didn't even bat an eye. It was "her" counter, and she didn't like anyone else back there – including me.

Brody leaned forward on both forearms and looked at us. "Okay, well…we know the murder happened sometime after the council meeting last night. And we know that Tom was trying to delay the vote on the new streets on the south side of town. He used some parliamentary procedure to stop the vote last night so he could set up a hearing where the townspeople could voice their opinion – which he was trying to sway in opposition to the project. He had pamphlets made up and everything."

"That's right. Red said they set the meeting for this Saturday afternoon," Deloris said.

"Right. So, besides the council members and the mayor, there were only a handful of people at the meeting – Red, Pastor D'Arnaud, Hattie Harper and Sandy Skitter from the Ladies' Aid group, Liz Farber from the salon, and Ronnie Towns from the hardware store."

"Well, you don't think Red did it, do you, Sheriff?" Junior asked with a concerned look.

Deloris shook her head. "Of course not. Red left the meeting early and took me to see a movie."

We all looked at her with stunned amazement. Red had a crush on Deloris for a long time, but she always spurned his advances.

"What? I was wanting to see that *Atomic Blonde,* and Red offered to take me to Ballers Ferry to see it. I don't like driving that far at night. Get your minds out of the gutter."

It was hard to tell for sure, but from the look on her face, the gutter might have been the right place for our minds. Brody continued:

"I don't really think any of them did it, but we're still checking out their alibis."

"My money is on Liz," Deloris said.

"Deloris!" I couldn't believe she was blaming our hairdresser for Tom's murder. "She's our friend, and she does your hair twice a month."

"Yep…and I've never heard her say a good word about anyone, unless they were standing right in front of her. And I told ya, that dumpster smelled like Tom just had his toenails done when we first looked at the body."

Everybody started talking at once until Brody whistled and waved his arms.

"I don't have time to discuss everybody's theories right now," Brody said, taking back control of the conversation. "Most of the people who came to see the meeting live in the new part of town on the hill and are opposed to the project, like Tom, anyway. We'll check the alibis of everyone who attended, including Liz. But the council members all had an interest in getting it approved. So, they may have had a motive."

"I don't know about that," Jake said, shaking his head.

"Well, I have to start somewhere. Today I want to start with those on the council who have a clear motive – in particular, the Mayor and Joan Pianowski. Bud lives in that part of town and owns a lot of empty lots there, and Joan runs the Realty House and has a bunch of rental houses there – so they both want the street upgrade to go through so their property values will go up and they will be more attractive to renters and buyers."

There were a lot of concerned eyes at the counter.

"Look, I know these people are your friends, and you grew up with them," Brody said, "but somebody choked Tom Hopkins to death…"

"Choked him!" Jake and Junior said in unison.

"Oops…well, that's not supposed to be public information. Don't forget – you're sworn to secrecy."

"We're strong supporters of law enforcement, Sheriff. We're not going to tell anyone," Pete Jenkins told him.

"Yeah," Junior agreed, "unless we accidentally blurt it out like you just did."

Brody sighed and was only partially successful in holding back an eye roll. He took a breath and opened his mouth to say something to Junior, but then shook it off. "Okay, well, we still have more of these dumpster fires going on. If we find who's starting the fires, we'll find the killer. The fires mostly moved out of Paint Creek to the surrounding towns yesterday afternoon and evening, but there was one behind Towns' End Hardware at 10 o'clock this morning."

"Wow, in broad daylight," I said. "I guess our fire here was in the morning yesterday, but that takes a lot of nerve. So…what can I do to help?"

"Eyes and ears. I need you to do a stakeout."

"A stakeout?" I wasn't thrilled with the idea. "You mean like sitting in a second-story room with binoculars and a camera?"

"No!" Junior said excitedly. "We'll need a spy truck! You know…one of those big vans with listening equipment for the bugs we plant in the big party room with big marble staircases on both sides, during a big charity fund-raising event for the arts. All the big mobsters will be there. You'll go inside in an alluring gown, with your hair in curls and cherry bomb red lipstick, wearing X-ray eyeglasses with a camera and heat vision, and you'll have a pistol in you garter just above the knee. And I'll be in the van watching it all on 10 big monitors and talking to you in your earpiece. And then you'll engage the prince in a little flirty chatter and…"

"Whoa, whoa, whoa there, Junior!" Brody was flabbergasted at Junior's imagination. "This isn't *Mission Impossible* or *James Bond*. This is about dumpster fires and a murder in Paint Creek, Kentucky. I'm talking about a stakeout, sitting in your car with binoculars and a camera, keeping track of Ms. Pianowski and the Mayor's wife, Elena. Her brother-in-law has submitted a bid for the work, and one of the council members told me in confidence that Elena asked the mayor to show her the competing bids so he can have the inside track."

"Hmm," I said, "I like Junior's idea better. There's a gown in the Calhoun Mall that I'd love to bill to my McLean County expense account."

Brody was getting a little impatient, so I decided to behave. "A stakeout sounds fine, Brody. When? Where?"

"Maybe from like 6:00 to 9:00 or 10:00 today

and tomorrow, for starters. But I don't want you out there alone. Maybe Pete can go with you. What do you think, Pete?"

"As long as we're done by 10:00…"

"I'll do it." Junior volunteered.

Yikes. Please, no, no, no… "But you and your dad have that construction project coming up later today…"

"That's not a problem, Mercy," his dad said. "It's just a garage door. I'll get Zack to help me. You need Junior with you because of all the investigating we've already done on the case."

"But, Jake, I think Zack might have football practice this afternoon…"

"Summer practice doesn't begin for two more weeks…uh…" Brody immediately realized his mistake when he saw the darts flying out of my eyes. "I mean, yeah, maybe he has practice."

"Zack!" Jake hollered into the kitchen. "You wanna make twenty bucks for helping me for about an hour or so around supper time today?"

"Twenty bucks! Yeah…sure! It takes me three hours to make that much around this place."

"It's settled then, Mercy. You need the best man for the job, and you got him. Junior, you go ahead and share everything we've found out with Mercy when you're out there."

Oh, joy. "Yay! I can hardly wait, Junior." I felt sick to my stomach. I like Junior, but I don't know if I can spend three or four hours alone with him without pulling my hair out.

"We'll take your little roadster, Mercy. It looks more like a spy car than my Rav. I'm going to go home and get cleaned up and ready. See you soon!"

Chapter Nine

I felt as conspicuous as a woman in a men's room as I pulled into the big corner parking lot across the street from the Realty House in beautiful downtown Paint Creek. My classic 1957 silver blue Mercedes roadster convertible always attracted attention, so it was difficult to try to be incognito. It was a few minutes before 6:00, and the sun wouldn't set until 9:00.

I had a good view of the comings and goings at Joan Pianowski's office, and I could also see the little children's dance studio upstairs of the barbershop next to it. At night they had spinning classes, yoga, and Pilates up there, and tonight Bud and Elena Finster were expected to be there for their weekly ballroom dance class. It was becoming very popular with the seniors in town.

I put the top up on my convertible to have a little more privacy and looked at my watch. I told Junior to meet me here at 6:00, and I saw his Toyota Rav4 coming down Main Street, right on time.

I held back feelings of dread and nausea that tried to overtake me. *You owe me big time, Brody Hayes.*

Junior waved at me and parked his car on the street right in front of my position in the lot, blocking my view of everything. *Good start.* He got out of the car, and I couldn't believe what I saw. He was in a black suit, black fedora, and dark aviator sunglasses, looking more like the chubby Blues Brother than a Man in Black. He was carrying a white box and had a serious look on his face as he opened the passenger door and got in.

"Good evening, Agent Howard. Did Sheriff Hayes give you the binoculars and camera?"

"Got 'em, 007. What's in the box?"

He looked at me as if he couldn't believe I didn't know, and opened the cover on the box.

"Well, this is a stakeout, so I brought the donuts. I'm pretty sure they're required." He pulled one out that was covered in powdered sugar and took a bite. The white cloud he created slowly settled onto his black suit. "I got some girly ones with strawberry frosting and sprinkles for you, Mercy."

"How thoughtful of you, Junior. But I think I'll wait a while." I wanted to feel indignant about the "girly" remark, but I really did love strawberry frosting with sprinkles. My waistline mocked me as I looked longingly inside the donut box.

The more he brushed the powdered sugar off

his suit, the worse it looked, but he didn't seem to mind. "Why did you park here, Mercy? We can't see across the street?"

I gave him a sarcastic look and then turned my head toward his car.

"Oh! Maybe I should move my car."

Ya think? "That might be a good idea, Junior."

Before he could get out of the car, I noticed people on the street waving to us as they passed by, and more cars were coming into the lot for ballroom dancing and haircuts. The barbershop was open late on Thursdays.

"On second thought, Junior. Just leave your car where it is." I got out of the car and motioned for him to do the same. I went around to his side of the car and put the donuts, fedora, and sunglasses inside on the seat. "Why don't you leave your suit jacket here too? It's a warm night...you'll be too hot."

"Where are we going?" He reluctantly took off his suit jacket, covered in powdered sugar, and put it in the car.

The parking lot was right next to Julia Ridley's little coffee shop, Moonbucks, which had a big picture window in the front. "We're going to sit at the window in the coffee shop. We'll have a perfect view and won't draw as much attention to ourselves."

"But how are people going to know we're spies if they don't see me in my spy suit?"

Maybe Junior didn't understand the concept of spying very well.

"It's all in the attitude on your face and the confidence in your walk, Junior." I gave him a steely look. "Let's go. Head up, and strut like you're on a mission."

I took his big arm in both of my hands, and we walked across the lot. Just as we approached the corner of the coffee shop, two teenagers on bicycles came zooming around from the sidewalk and almost ran us down. They kept going right through the lot and then around the back of the building into the alley.

"Kids these days!" Junior said. "Do you know who they were, Mercy?"

"Not sure. They both had baseball caps on, and their heads were down, so the visor blocked my view."

"The second one was a girl, Merse."

"Really?"

"It was a girl's bike, and she had a bun under

her cap. Plus, she was wearing flowery perfume."

I was impressed. And there was a hint of perfume in the air. "That's a pretty good observation there, Detective. Too bad we're not here to stakeout kids on bicycles."

It was fairly busy downtown at this time of day. There was a lot of foot traffic, with people heading for the gym and barbershop or picking up a few last-minute items at the grocery store for dinner. The ATM in the bank lobby, a few doors down from the barbershop, seemed to be busy as well, and people who were at the office during the day were stopping into the Realty House too. The after-work crowd was also in full-force here at Moonbucks, sipping on coffee and chatting with friends.

"We better grab two stools at the window before we get in line, Junior."

"Sit down, sit down!" a friendly voice said behind me. It was shop owner, Julia Ridley. "I haven't seen you here in ages, Mercy! Hi, Junior! Are you two…together now? I thought you and the Sheriff…" She was trying to hide her disbelief behind a smile.

"Junior and I? Oh, Julia…"

"Yes, Ms. Ridley…Mercy is my fiancé."
Junior was getting his steely spy face down a little

too well.

Julia gasped.

"Oh, he's just kidding, Julia. I'm still with Brody. We just thought we'd come here to talk about a project I have in mind, adding a little shed to my garage. It's hard to get anything accomplished at the diner…so many distractions and interruptions when it's your own place. You know how it is."

She looked relieved. "Of course, Mercy. We'll have to catch up soon."

"Absolutely – stop by for lunch sometime. Say, I hear you might be getting a fancy new coffee machine."

"Well, I don't know. I'm going to look at a couple tomorrow. But the younger set in Paint Creek is starting to demand their lattes and espressos, you know. Coffee, Mercy?"

"Yes, please – give me the bottomless cup. I'll grab some cream from the condiment bar. Junior?"

He had his nose wrinkled and a concerned expression. "Do I have to drink coffee on a stakeout?"

"And lemonade for Junior – a pitcher."

Julia went to get our order herself, as the baristas were swamped.

"So, how come you ruined my story about us being engaged? It was a great cover story."

"Yes, it would have been a good cover, Junior. But Brody and I run into Julia fairly often at the country club, so it would have seemed suspicious."

He bobbled his head from side to side. "Whatever. And I didn't know you wanted some work done on your garage. I thought you had plenty of room in there."

"That was our cover story, Junior."

He thought for a second. "Oh…I get it. I'm in construction, and you have a garage."

We had only been sipping on our beverages for a minute when something across the street caught Junior's eye. "Hey, the mayor's wife just came out of the real estate place…"

I looked and saw Elena. She turned and looked back to the real estate office, and her husband came out to join her. "And Bud is right behind her. Looks like he's still chatting with Joan inside."

"There they go now, upstairs to the yoga

place."

*That's interesting. Maybe Joan is in cahoots
with Bud and Elena. I really hope not.*

"Fire! Fire!"

Everyone stood up immediately, ready to make
their escape, as a young worker ran in the back
door hollering about a fire.

"No, no! It's outside, in the dumpster," he
said. "It's not close to the building…sorry…sit
down, you guys."

Julia grabbed the fire extinguisher from the
wall mount and followed him back out the door
toward the alley. Junior and I followed. The fire
must have been burning for several minutes, and
the flames leapt high above the dumpster. Julia
sprayed it with the extinguisher, but it was too hot
to get close. She could only spray the flames
above the dumpster and not the garbage that was
burning inside. The defiant flames continued their
haughty dance.

"I got this," Junior said calmly. He pulled a
juice carton out of the bag of garbage that the
worker had dropped when he saw the fire and
used it protect his hand from the hot dumpster lid.
He lifted the cover, bending away from the heat,
and let it slam down on the flaming trash bin. The
flames curled out around the edges of the lid for a

moment and then subsided. Then Junior lifted the lid halfway and motioned with his head for Julia give it a shot with the extinguisher.

"Stan is on his way," I said. "Do we need to call the fire department?"

"Don't call the emergency line, Merse," Junior said. "Stan will get someone here to make sure it's not going to start burning again. They've got it down to a system now. And they want to preserve things for the, you know, science guys."

Maybe Junior had been doing his homework on these fires.

"What are these?" I asked, looking at some marks on the tar in front of the dumpster.

"Looks like skid marks from a bicycle…or two," Junior said. "They had been going pretty fast and then slammed on their brakes right in front of the dumpster. Looks like some tread marks in the gravel over there when they were riding away."

Junior and I looked at each other. *Maybe we should have been here to stakeout teenagers on bicycles.*

Chapter Ten

It had been such a stressful few days, so I decided to come home after the breakfast rush was over. I needed time to relax and think about all of the details that seemed to be coming at me at 100 miles an hour. The fire, the body, the autopsy evidence, the council connection, the other fires, the mayor and his wife at Joan Pianowski's office, and then the fire at Julia's coffee shop. Were two teenagers on bicycles really our murderers? I just couldn't make sense out of it all. The pieces just didn't seem to fit. Something was missing.

I called Brody and asked him to stop by when he had a chance, and he said wanted to talk to me about the stakeout too and would be by in a couple hours.

I threw in a load of laundry and then sat on the tufted armchair in the living room. "So, who killed Tom Hopkins and started all those fires, Wizard?"

His theories were worse than Junior's.

"No, I don't think some guy from Indiana just decided to swoop into Paint Creek and randomly kill somebody and create havoc in our little town – although that would explain why the evidence doesn't paint a nice cohesive picture."

My cell phone rang as I paused to actually consider the possibility that this was all just a random crime spree. It was Ruby calling, and that made me smile. "Hello there, girl."

"Hi, neighbor! I saw your car in the driveway, and thought you might want to…"

"…find out the juicy details of your date with Troy last night. Yes! Come on over."

"Are you sure? I don't want to bother you if you've got things to do."

"Please, come over, Ruby. I need someone to talk to – and bring your dog. I'd like to meet him."

"Oh, I don't know. I mean, she's been professionally trained, but…"

"Just bring him…uh, her! The coffee is ready."

Ten seconds later, the doorbell rang. *That can't be Brody yet…* I opened the door with a curious look still on my face.

"Ruby! That was fast."

"Well, I called when I saw your car, just as we were getting back from our walk, so I just came right here instead of going home first. This is Goldie."

"Oh! Come in," I said, a bit cautiously. "Your 'little pooch' is a full-size golden retriever."

"She's a Yellow Labrador, actually. Golden Retrievers usually have longer fur, and I'm pretty sure that Labs are smarter. Yeah, I kind of figured you were expecting a little Chihuahua in my purse."

"I guess I was." Goldie was still on her leash, so I opened the door all the way. "Hopefully she doesn't have a taste for Hamsters!"

"Don't worry, Wizard and Gracie are safe! Put out your open palm and let her sniff it. Goldie, this is my friend, Mercy."

Goldie sniffed my hand and then kind of did a little sneeze and licked my hand.

"There…okay now, shake hands…now you're friends for life. She'll never forget you – and since you're my friend, she'll protect you too. Goldie, sit…stay."

She sat obediently by the front door as we moved to the sofa.

"So, you wear a dress to walk your dog?"

"I like dresses. They're comfortable – and I'm a girl!"

Yes, and I'm a "ma'am."

Goldie whimpered once as we sat down.

"Okay, you can lie down, Goldie," Ruby told her.

"Oh, let her come over and lie by our feet. She's one of the girls."

One nod from her master, and Goldie was there.

I had the thermal pot and two cups on the coffee table, and I poured the steamy beverage. I also set out a handful of vanilla wafers on a glass serving plate, and picked one up.

"These aren't your family recipe, Rube, but they're great for dunking. So – dish, girl! How was your date?"

"It was…nice."

"Not exactly a ringing endorsement, Ruby."

"No! I mean…it was really nice. Troy's a great guy. He has a lot of samples of restaurant equipment in his car, but he cleaned out the front seat for me."

"Well, that was nice of him…"

"He spent a lot of time texting on his phone at first trying to cancel a delivery or something, but he couldn't get a hold of them. But then he let it go, and we had a good time. We had a bite to eat at a really fun little burger place on the way. Then we had a couple Margaritas and danced at the club he brought me to. It seems like he knows everybody wherever he goes, and everybody knows him too. I met some really nice people."

"And afterwards…?"

"Well, the moon was almost full, and he knew this place with a beautiful view at night, overlooking a lake with the moonlight reflecting on the ripples. It was beautiful."

"Mmhm." I paused and gave her a look that she understood. "And…?"

"Well, there might have been a little kissing."

"Yes! Okay, Ruby…details!"

She looked like she was getting a little uncomfortable, but friends talk about everything, right? Okay, so we've only been friends for a day, but still.

Then the doorbell rang.

"Oh, crud."

Ruby smiled and let out a sigh of relief. "Saved by the bell!"

I opened the door.

"Brody! That was a short couple of hours. Come in!" I gave him a kiss on the cheek, and he gave me a nice squeeze. "I wasn't expecting you for a while yet."

"Well, I thought it would probably be better to talk to you first before I stop at Moonbucks."

"Hi, Brody," Ruby greeted him. "You're going to Moonbucks? That's where Troy should be right now, so give him some time to sell her a new coffee machine."

"And maybe a new security system, after what happened last night," I added. "I'll tell you about it in a while, Ruby."

Brody got two steps inside before Goldie was sitting at attention by Ruby and letting out a low growl. Ruby started to introduce Goldie to Brody, but I cut her off and shook my head.

"This is Ruby's dog, Goldie, Brody. She only likes special people." I got down on one knee, hugged her neck, and let her lick my face. "Isn't that right, girl?"

I stood up, and Brody put his arm around me, which got another growl and one bark from my new protector.

"She can probably smell the treachery in your heart, Brody."

He tried to reach out to pet Goldie's head, but she let out some more controlled but scary growls and barks. Then he held out his open palm to her.

"Hi, there, Goldie. I'm Brody."

She sniffed, sneezed, and licked, and then she let him pet her head.

"How did you know what to do, Mr. Smarty Pants?"

"I was a dog in a past life."

Just don't let me find out you're a dog in this life too…

The conversation turned to the investigation, of course, and I told Brody and Ruby everything I could remember about my stakeout with Junior last night.

Ruby looked distraught. "That's so scary, Mercy. I thought Paint Creek would be an idyllic little paradise."

"It is," I assured her, putting my hand on hers. "I grew up here, and this is just a passing fluke."

"We're getting it figured out, Ruby." Brody was coming back from the refrigerator with a small bottle of apple juice.

"It's looks like you feel pretty much at home

here, Sheriff." Ruby said with a sly grin. "I guess you must be spending a lot of time here."

"Oh, no – I'm the Sheriff. I do this at everybody's house."

"Right."

"But anyway, ladies, there have been sightings of kids on bikes around three or four of the fires in the towns around here. And we got some information back from the lab on the evidence from some of the dumpsters."

"Is this a gang of killers on bicycles? Or what?"

"I really doubt it. If there was an MS13 gang around here, or something like that, we'd be seeing a lot more brutal and bloody crimes of violence. I just can't figure out why there was one body in the first fire and then a dozen more fires with no bodies."

"Yeah," that was befuddling me too, "It's not like the other fires are going to draw attention away from the murder. And the more fires they start, the more clues they leave and the better chance they have of getting caught."

"Exactly."

Chapter Eleven

Ruby crossed her legs and sipped her coffee as the conversation continued. That caught Brody's eye, and I saw him look her up and down in that way that guys do without even being aware that they're doing it.

"So, what have you learned from the crime scene investigators, Sheriff?" she asked. "You said you've seen some results."

The doorbell rang again, and I got up to see who it was. "My goodness, it's like Grand Central Station around here today!"

It was Deloris. She ran home from the diner for an emergency hairspray application and decided to stop by to say hello to Gracie. For some reason, she liked her more than my little Wizard. Apparently, Goldie likes all women and didn't pay any attention.

"Sit down, Deloris. Coffee? Brody was just going to tell us some new information about the investigation."

"I already told you, Mercy, it was Liz who did it. And I don't drink coffee after I've had my first shot of bourbon. It kills my buzz, and people get stupider and more annoying again."

"Oh! Okay, then." Ruby and I looked at each

other. "Well, I'm sure Liz was still at her salon last night when the fire started at the coffee house. We're pretty sure it was some kids on bicycles."

"Maybe," Brody added.

"Well, then Liz put them up to it. What's the new information, Sheriff?"

"Well, there's not a lot. But they found some fibers in front of some of the dumpsters involved…and inside some of the dumpsters where the fires were put out quickly or didn't burn very well. There were a few of these fibers along with the soot and ashes on Tom Hopkins' suit jacket too."

"What kind of fibers?" Ruby asked.

"That's the thing. They were mostly cotton or cotton blends, but they were not all from the same garment or carpet or whatever. They were mostly small, short fibers in a variety of colors, different thicknesses, different fabrics. There doesn't seem to be a single source. There's some Egyptian cotton from sheets, fuzz from sweatshirts, and even hair from lots of different people. Fur from cats and dogs too."

"That's weird. So, did they use gasoline to get the fires going, or what?" Deloris asked.

"No. In many of the fires, the accelerant used

was the charcoal lighter fluid people use in their grills. But wherever the fibers were found – including the fire at the diner, Mercy – the accelerant was acetone."

"Bingo!" Deloris said triumphantly. "Ha! That's why it smelled like a manicure when we found Tom. Acetone is nail polish remover, and Liz has plenty of that around her salon."

"Well, it's pretty readily available," Brody pointed out.

"And everybody has a bottle," I added. "Liz doesn't exactly use it by the drum load."

The buzzer went off on my washer in the mud room by the back door.

"Back in a minute, guys. There's more coffee in the pot. I'm going to toss my clothes into the dryer."

I had to fight the urge to holler out to Wizard, because we usually have a conversation while I'm doing the laundry. My loads are pretty eclectic, since it's just me. I hand wash a few things and keep my whites separate, but otherwise it's a load of durables and a load of delicates.

I shook out the pairs of my shorts, tops, and a couple of floral pillow cases and tossed them in the dryer. *I better clean the lint trap…it's been a few loads.*

I pulled out the strip of grey lint, speckled with colors, and set it on top of the dryer while I set the timer and turned it on. Then I balled up the lint and picked it up to put it in the kitchen trash. Of course, a lot of loose lint stayed on the machine, and I wiped it off with a sponge I kept on the utility sink. *Mental note: Get some more small trash bags for the laundry room.*

In the middle of the kitchen, it dawned on me, and I brought the ball of lint into the living room. "Look what I've got here," I announced, holding out the lint ball on my open hand.

"What's that, Mercy?" Brody asked.

"It better not be a dead mouse, or I'm outta here," Deloris stated firmly.

"No," I said, "it's just…"

"The lint from your dryer?" Ruby asked, looking at me like I'd lost my mind.

"Yes, dryer lint." They waited politely for me to elaborate and convince them I wasn't crazy. "You know…a bunch of small fibers of different shapes, sizes, colors, and fabrics. And there's probably a little bit of hamster fur in here too, and a couple of long blonde hairs from yours truly."

Brody put on a thoughtful squint and started to nod slowly. "So, maybe the fibers were just from garbage that people had thrown away."

"Nonsense. There's no dryer at the diner and most of these other places." Deloris took the last vanilla wafer off the serving plate and pulled a Bic lighter out of her beehive. "Bring that thing over here, Mercy. Is this plate crystal?"

"Just glass."

"Good. Set it on here." She put the plate with the ball of lint on the coffee table. "Hold onto your beast there, Ruby."

Then she flicked the lighter and held the flame to the dryer lint. A big flame rose a foot off the plate, and in a few seconds the ball was gone.

"Maybe not just garbage, Sheriff," she said. "Looks like some mighty good kindling to me."

Ruby suddenly seemed agitated and uncomfortable, and she stood up. "Goldie and I have to get going – thanks for the coffee and cookies, Mercy."

She headed for the door, and I ran to open it for her. "Is everything all right?" I whispered to her.

"I'm fine," she said. Then she turned to the

others. "Bye, Deloris. And, Sheriff…why don't you try to get to the coffee shop before Troy leaves. Ask him to meet us all at the diner for lunch."

"Well, I'm not sure I'll have time for lunch with everybody…"

"Please," she said firmly with a serious look in her eye.

This didn't have the feel of a casual social request. We all had a quiet moment, and then Brody nodded and responded. "Of course, Ruby. I'll tell him. We'll be there."

Ruby gave me a strained smile and then was out the door.

"That woman's got something up her sleeve," Deloris said.

I was still stunned and my eyes were frozen on the door. I answered mindlessly, "Her dress doesn't have sleeves."

Chapter Twelve

Troy had not arrived at the diner yet, but Brody, Ruby, and I had started to discuss the dumpster fires in a four-top booth.

"The fire at Moonbucks last night was the last fire," Brody said. "There weren't any overnight, and there haven't been any reported this morning, so maybe they're over."

Red turned around on his stool at the counter. "Maybe the killer moved on to another area."

"Or he figured that he started enough fires to cover up the murder," Jake added.

"Or he ran out of money, 'cause the printing press is probably gone by now," Junior said through a mouthful of spaghetti and meatballs.

Babs put all of our beverages back on her tray. "You better move to the big table, because everyone wants to get in on this conversation, guys." She took the coffee and soft drinks away and set them up on the long table where the guys have their meetings and post-ballgame gatherings.

Brody rolled his eyes. "This is official law enforcement business, Mercy. Does the whole town have to be in on it?"

"You deputized all of us, Sheriff," Junior said as he picked up his plate and headed for the table. "Remember?"

"We're deputies?" Red asked, a little confused.

"You weren't here," Jake told him. "It's just us

and the ladies."

"And me," Pete Jenkins said as he took a seat at the table.

Red looked a little disheartened and stayed at the counter.

"Come on, Red," I told him. "You're a deputy too – right, Brody?"

Brody shrugged. "Sure…why not?"

We all got seated and settled, and I got everyone up to date on our stakeout observations, the fire at the coffee shop, and the fibers. Deloris told them about her experiment with the dryer lint.

"And," I added, "if you've ever set a ball of lint on top of your dryer, you all know how easily it sheds loose little fibers."

"Okay," Brody said as the update wound down, and then he looked at Ruby. "So, why are we all here, Ruby? You seemed to have something on your mind when you left Mercy's."

She slowly looked around at everyone and exhaled. "Well, you know I was out with Troy last night…"

"Oh, for mercy sake," Red said. "Are we going to talk about dating now?"

"Why 'mercy sake,' Red?" I asked, not liking my name involved.

"Because it's about time that people stop saying 'for Pete's sake' all the time," Pete Jenkins interjected.

Point taken.

"Hush, now," Deloris said, heading back behind the counter to set out some plates of hot food for Babs. "Let the woman talk. Tell them what you have to say, Ruby."

"So…I told you that his car was full of restaurant equipment, and so he had to move some things to the trunk. He took a box of security cameras off the front seat, and I grabbed some loose pamphlets and followed him. There was a big clear plastic bag, like the ones a new coffee maker or TV comes in when you take it out of the box."

Or a soda machine or cappuccino machine, I thought.

"It was filled with grey fuzz – dryer lint. I asked him why he had it in his trunk, and he said it was from the laundry machines he has in the laundromat and apartment buildings. He said he takes it out of the buildings because it's a fire hazard."

That got everybody buzzing.

"But wait," Ruby insisted, "there's more. After I left your house this morning, Mercy, I got to thinking about the timing of the fires. He had an appointment here Thursday morning, the day after your dumpster fire on Wednesday."

"I set that appointment up with him on Tuesday, after lunch," Deloris said from the corner of the counter.

Ruby continued. "Then he had an appointment at Moonbucks for this morning, and they had a fire last night."

Junior scratched his head. "So, why would he want to burn the place down before he goes there?"

"To sell security systems," I said, and Ruby nodded. "It's like the auto glass guy you were telling me about, Ruby. He shot out windshields at night and then made a fortune fixing them the next day."

"Yeah," Jake said. "That makes sense. There was a tire guy in Akron that got caught slashing tires at night a few years back."

"And then there was that time," Junior said, "that we drove our truck over Red's old tool shed when he wasn't home, and he had us build him a new one."

Jake gave him a disturbed look, but it was Red who responded.

"You brain-dead fool," Red said. "I told your dad to tear it down and build me a new one before he knocked it over."

Pete Jenkins got things back on track. "That Troy guy stopped into Town's end Hardware the day after the fire in the dumpster there too," he told us, "and Ronnie bought some security cameras and a few cases of some kind of fire-suppressant pods that he's selling there now."

Junior held up one finger for us to wait for his comment as he slurped down the last of his milkshake. "And he does his own installations and plumbing. He'd have plenty of acetone-based solvents to clean rubber cement or other adhesives and gunk off plastic pipes for drains he was fixing."

Everyone paused for a moment to soak it all in.

"It seems like you have a pretty good group of deputies, Brody," I said with smile, and he nodded in agreement.

Troy Stargill walked in the front door, and the diner grew silent as all eyes turned to him. He looked to see if there was somebody behind him that they might all be looking at and then checked the zipper on his pants.

"Come here, Troy," Ruby said, patting the seat of the chair next to her. "I saved a spot for you."

I tried to break the awkward silence as he sat down. "So, did Julia buy a coffee machine, Troy?"

"Top of the line!" He said with his big bright smile, "Dual espresso heads, dual steamer bars with 18 bars of pressure each, a built-in full-pound heavy-duty burr grinder, and a 2000-watt fully integrated thermo-coil heating system. That puppy will put out 480 cups of perfect coffee every hour for 20 years! I'd have been here sooner, but she wanted me to install some security cameras too." He leaned over to give Ruby a kiss on the cheek, but she pulled her head away.

A dark-haired girl, about 15 years old, walked in and looked around the diner. It was Ketty Fike. Her family lived a couple of blocks from me. She spotted Troy and walked over to him.

"Hi, Mister. I saw your car out front. We made that delivery for you last night, so you owe us ten bucks. Can I get that now? And maybe a bonus again, because I saw that she bought…some more things."

I noticed the scent of a familiar floral perfume as she stood by the table, and I watched Troy as his face grew white.

"Uh…" Troy saw us all looking at him intently and tried to get rid of her. "Stop by the Tastee Freeze in an hour, and I'll take care of you, honey."

She looked displeased and turned to leave.

"Ketty," I said, and waited for her to come back to the table.

"Yes, Miss Howard?"

"That 'delivery' you did for Mr. Stargill last night…it wouldn't have been a dumpster fire at Moonbucks, would it? You almost hit me with your bicycle shortly before the fire there."

Her eyes nearly popped out of her head, and she turned slightly, contemplating a run for the exit. Then she started shaking.

"I just remembered I have an appointment in Calhoun," Troy said, getting up from his chair.

"Sit down," Brody told him in an authoritative, macho tone that gave me a little thrill. Troy sat.

"You're not going to tell my parents, are you?" she asked, her arms hanging limply at her sides and tears streaming down her face.

Ruby stood up, stroked the girl's back gently, and spoke calmly. "No, we're not going to tell your parents, sweetheart." She smiled, and Ketty raised her head. "You are."

Ketty stopped crying, and her eyes grew wide. Then she nodded slowly. She looked at Brody. "He offered us a lot of money to do five dumpsters, and said to just call it a delivery when we texted him that each one was done. I really wanted money for some shoes I saw at Carlson's downtown…but nobody will hire me because I'm not 16."

"I'll hire you, Ketty," I said. She's bright, and a good kid. "An hour a day at lunchtime clearing tables. Minimum wage. You can start tomorrow."

I could see the excitement fill her eyes as a hint of a smile grew on her face. She nodded, and then turned slowly toward Brody. "Do I have to go to jail, Sheriff Hayes?"

"I doubt it, Miss…uh, Ketty. But you will have to tell us everything. Come to my office at the Village Hall tomorrow at noon – or when you're done clearing tables here – and bring your friend on the other bike. That has to happen if you don't want to be in trouble with the law. Do you understand?"

She nodded and then looked back at Ruby.

"Who are you? You're really pretty."

Ruby smiled. "I'm your history teacher, Ketty. I think you're really going to like my class." Then she gave the girl a hug, and Ketty left the diner.

Brody got up from his chair, speaking as he rose. "Okay, Mr. Stargill. you can stand up now. His handcuffs jingled as he pulled them from the pouch on his utility belt.

Troy stood, looking very glum and deflated. He turned and put his arms behind his back.

"Can I do it, Sheriff?" Junior asked. "Can I cuff him? I'm a deputy."

"I'll take care of it, Junior," Brody answered him and then read Troy his rights.

"So, how come you killed Tom Hopkins?" Junior asked. "I don't get it."

"Oh, no you don't!" Troy said, suddenly very animated. "You're not going to pin that murder on me! I never even knew the guy. I didn't even know there was a body in the dumpster when I…I…I want a lawyer." Then he looked at Ruby. "I'm not a killer, babe. You believe me, don't you? This is all just a big misunderstanding."

"Oh, I believe you," Ruby said. "I mean, you

practically fainted when you found out about the body. And I called *Bangers* – you were there the night that man was killed."

Troy seemed relieved. "So, we're okay, then? We'll get through this, and it'll be like none of this every happened."

"No, Troy. It'll be like *we* never happened."

"But I'm not a killer!"

"No, you're not a killer. You're just a thug with no soul who endangers lives, makes a whole town live in fear, and destroys property so you can try to scam people out of their money."

"But, it's all top-quality security equipment that they should really have."

"Save your sales pitch, Troy. The problem isn't with your equipment; it's with you. You're a con artist and a common criminal. You no doubt handle the rest of your life and your relationships with the same lack of morality that you use to run your business."

Brody had called his deputy, Stan Doggerty, to come to the diner, and he walked in the front door.

"Deputy Dawg!" Red greeted him. "Sheriff has a present for you, cuffed and ready to go."

"Holding tank in Calhoun, Sheriff?" Stan asked.

"Yep. Frisk him, just in case. Oh – and he asked for an attorney, so no interrogation until he has one."

"Yes, sir. What am I charging him with?"

"Arson with intent to defraud, for now. We'll add more charges when I get back."

Babs and Deloris came to the table with several plates of food.

"Okay guys!" Babs sang sweetly, "Lunch is served! Eat well – we still have a murder to solve!"

Chapter Thirteen

This was beginning to feel like the longest week of my life. Tom was killed some time after the town council meeting on Tuesday night; the first dumpster fire was started by Troy Stargill at the Old School Diner on Wednesday morning; and the last fire was started by his young minions on Thursday evening. Then, this morning we solved the dumpster fires (thanks to Ruby!), but it seems like we're back to square one on the murder.

I was helping Smoke rinse off the last of the dinner dishes and run them through the dishwasher when my cell phone rang.

"Hey, Mercy…it's Ruby. I've been texting you, but you never answer!"

"Sorry, girl…been in the kitchen, and it's a little noisy. What's up?"

"It's Friday night, and you need to relieve some stress. I'm taking you out."

"Out? Mmmm…I'm not dressed, I'm tired, my hair's a rat's nest, and I promised Wizard and Grace that I'd watch a movie with them tonight."

"Mercy Howard! You're 33 years old, active, beautiful, and worn out from this whole murder and dumpster fire thing. You need a night out, and you're not going to stand me up for two hamsters who couldn't pick you out of a lineup of refrigerators and grizzly bears."

Wizard knows me…doesn't he? I knew she was right about needing a night out, but I really didn't feel like doing anything too fancy. "Okay…but here's the deal. We'll just stay in Paint Creek and go to the Legion Club."

"The Legion Club? You mean like old geezers with no teeth who smoke, do the polka, and play pull tabs all night?"

"It's not quite that grim, Ruby. They just remodeled it last year, and they have a live combo there on the weekends."

She was skeptical. "Will we be…you know…popular there, with old geezers bothering us all the time?"

"Nope. Actually, Deloris and Babs are popular there. Most of the regulars are under 25 or over 50. Or on a date with their wife."

"Do they make a decent martini?"

I'm pretty sure no bartender there ever heard of a martini. "No, but they make a mean rum and Coke."

I could hear a hint of disgust in her sigh. "If I

hate it, we're leaving. I'll pick you up at home in an hour and a half."

*****

"I hate it."

Ruby wrinkled her nose as we walked into the Legion Club just before 10:00 p.m. I gave her my best sarcastic scowl, and led the way past the bar to a welcome of wolf whistles and hoots from the guys.

"I told you it would be horrible," she whispered to me.

"That's just how they welcome every woman who comes in the place. It's a tradition here."

"Welcome to 1955."

"It's no different than walking by a construction site in the city, Rube. Relax…don't let them smell your fear," I kidded.

"Hey there, Mercy!" the bartender greeted me. "Good to see you tonight."

"Hi, Earl. Looking pretty dapper tonight in your cowboy shirt. Two rum and Cokes."

Earl Rollins was a good ol' boy with a farm just west of town.

"Got a real nice little band tonight, Mercy. I think you'll like 'em. They'll be starting a new set in a few minutes," Earl said.

I think I heard Zack say that his group was playing tonight. They're all young guys, and he's the drummer.

Earl set two tall drinks on the bar and put a red straw in each one. "Here you go…my special recipe!"

"Let me guess, Earl…rum and, um…Coke?"

Ruby rolled her eyes and grabbed a wedge of lime from the garnish tray on the bar, so I grabbed a couple green olives and popped them in my mouth.

Earl winked and laughed. It was the same "joke" he had used for years, but he never got tired of it, and I was always happy to play along.

"Enjoy your evening, ladies."

I nodded and gave him a two-finger salute as we continued on to a small table, not too close to the stage. Gilbert Gallagher was playing pool with one hand across the room. One arm was still in a sling. His brother Dickie was sitting at a table near him, whittling, I think, which was his favorite pastime. They gave us a wave.

"I should introduce you around so your new neighbors can meet you, Ruby."

"Ha! It would seem like you're auctioning me off to the guy with the cheesiest pick-up line. No way."

I leaned in and looked her in the eye. "You live in Paint Creek now, Ruby. This is your life. You've got to get over your preconceived notions about rural guys being red necks and racist creeps. They're not. These are some of the sweetest, smartest guys you'll ever meet…and there isn't one of them who wouldn't stop to change your tire or give you the shirt off his back if you needed it."

She seemed skeptical but relaxed a little. "It's just that I'm used to…"

"…to lawyers and stockbrokers – the real self-absorbed narcissistic creeps. The guys here have other things on their minds besides getting into your pants." *Well…maybe not. She looks amazing in that red dress.*

"I don't wear pants, Mercy."

I gave her an incredulous look. She looked confused for a second and then slapped my arm.

"I'm not talking about *under*pants, you weirdo! I mean I always wear dresses!"

We laughed, and that seemed to break any remaining ice between her and the Legion Club.

"I was expecting this drink to be all booze so they could get us drunk, but it's made just right. I don't even need the lime," she said as the band took the stage. "Looks like polka time!"

Her jaw dropped when she heard the opening riff of *Layla* coming from the little stage.

"These guys aren't half bad," she said. "I mean, they're not Eric Clapton, but they have some early signs of talent. I'm going to go up and make some requests. I hope they know some Iron Maiden or Metallica."

"You're a head banger?" I asked as she ran off, turning to give me two quickly raised eyebrows. She had told me that means "yes" in Filipino.

After a long discussion with the guitarist they started playing something that sounded like Heavy Metal to me, and she came back to the table.

"Well," she said, "Guns 'n' Roses is as close as they can get for now, and *Welcome to the Jungle* is one of my favorites. I had to promise him that I'd go up and do Slash's guitar solo though, because he doesn't think he can do it justice."

I looked at her. "What?"

She took a good swig of her drink and got up again. "I'll be back."

She went up onto the stage and took the guitar from the guy who was singing. She kicked off her shoes, shook her hair like Janis Joplin, and then started to play. Every head in the house turned as she did an amazing guitar solo. When the song was over, she talked with the guys again. Then she gave back the guitar and grabbed the microphone. I couldn't believe it when she started singing.

Cold late night so long ago
When I was not so strong, you know...

She was singing *Magic Man* by Heart, one of my favorite songs of all time.

It seemed like he knew me.
He looked right through me...yeah...

The dance floor began to fill as the song continued.

Come on home girl, he said with a smile...

The song sounded every bit as good as the original.

But try to understand, try to understand
Try, try, try to understand...
He's a magic man

She went right into *Crazy on You,* air-drumming for Zack to get him to hit harder on the beat and showing him when to go into the transitional drum riffs. Then she came back to the table as the crowd roared and applauded. There were six more drinks waiting for her that people had sent over.

"Looks like you are popular here after all, Ruby. Who *are* you?"

She used a bar napkin from under one of the drinks to dab the sweat off her neck and forehead and took a sip of a drink as she caught her breath.

"Just a girl. Why?"

"Oh, no reason. I mean, not just anybody can get up on a stage, shred a guitar like Slash, and belt out a song like Ann Wilson."

"I used to play gigs with a band in college, but we were never able to get a record deal. My parents made me realize that you can't chase every dream, and teaching has been a dream of mine since I was a little girl."

Dickie Gilbert came over to the table with something in his hand. "Hi, Mercy. Hello, ma'am," he said to Ruby.

Hey! This time she's the ma'am!

"I just got finished carving this," he said, holding out a small figurine to Ruby. "It's an angel, and I want you to have it because you sing like an angel – or maybe a Hell's Angel," he said with a little snort. He turned to blow some sawdust and small wood shavings off the very detailed angel and then gave it to her.

Ruby was moved. "Well, thank you so much! I'm Ruby – Ruby Owana. I'm a new teacher at the high school."

"Dickie Gallagher," he said. His eyes beamed as they shook hands, as if he were meeting a movie star. "It's nice to meet you. Well, I'll go now – I'm sure you don't want a guy like me bothering you. Maybe I'll see you at the town meeting on the new streets at the Village Hall tomorrow, Mercy."

"That's tomorrow, Dickie?"

"Yep, 1:00 p.m." A few awkward bows, and he was gone.

"He's a sweet guy," she said, "and so shy. This angel is really beautiful."

"Let me see." She handed it to me, and I

looked at all of the intricate work in the angel's gown and wings. Even the face was very realistic. "Wow. You should stain and varnish it to keep it nice." I gave it back to her and wiped the fine, pasty wood dust off my thumb and fingers.

It was a very pleasant and relaxing evening with Ruby. I think she enjoyed the Legion Club even more than I did – and we never ran out of drinks. But, by the end of the evening my mind was spinning again with thoughts about the murder of Tom Hopkins. I felt like the solution to this terrible crime was staring me in the face, but I just couldn't put my finger on it.

Chapter Fourteen

It was a restless night of sleep for me, but I probably wouldn't have slept at all if it weren't for the three rum and Cokes I had at the Club. My mind had been twisting all through the night with the little bits of evidence and all the possible scenarios surrounding Tom's murder.

At the crack of dawn, my eyes popped open, and I bolted upright into a sitting position.

"I know who killed Tom Hopkins," I said out loud.

I got up and ran into the bathroom and started making a mental list of all the things I had to do to prove my theory.

"Wizard!" I hollered as I stepped into the shower, "Remind me to call Sylvia Chambers...What? Oh, she's the medical examiner...I thought you knew. And I have to stop by and see if Joan Pianowski is in her office this morning. That's right...the real estate lady. Call Brody for me, will you, Wizard? Never mind...I'll do it myself." I can't expect Wizard to do everything!

So many things to do...good thing I'm getting an early start. It was Saturday, so I had to pick up a nice beef roast at the butcher shop for Sunday dinner at Old School...oh, and some fresh ground beef. Ruby was going to want to drop off a nice fruit basket for Dickie too, as a thank you for the angel – *I'll put one together for her.* I was going to need some help from Deloris too. *Do I need Smoke for anything? How about Jake, Junior, and Red?*

I jumped out of the shower after less than 15 minutes, put my hair in a towel, and walked briskly past the vanity to my closet. I put on a dress, with the one o'clock meeting at the Village Hall in mind – and so I wouldn't look frumpy next to Ruby. I fed my babies and headed out of the house without making coffee. I would have a cup at Moonbucks, since I had to go to Joan Pianowski's office across the street from there. As I backed out of my driveway, I called Sylvia at her office, near the morgue in the county office building in Calhoun.

"Sylvia? Hi, it's Mercy Howard...I'm good, and you? Great! Say, did you get the results from the lab on that tan substance on Tom's collar by the blood stain? Uh huh...uh huh...Great, I thought so. And, Sylvia, do you have those pictures of the marks on Tom's body that looked like they might be impressions from a floor mat in the killer's trunk? Great, great...can you bring them to the town meeting in Paint Creek today at one o'clock? Oh...well, can you give the pictures to Brody this morning? He should be in his office there for another hour or two. What? Sure! I'll give you my email address, and you can send them right to me, if that's okay. Perfect!"

I parked in the corner lot by the coffee shop and went inside.

"Good morning, Mercy! Wow, I hadn't seen you for a month, and now here you are again, two times in one week!"

"Well, I'm on my way to see if Joan is in today at the Realty House – and I had to come and see your new super-duper deluxe coffee machine, Julia. It's real pretty – how do you like it so far?"

"Oh, I love it," she said, "I just wish I hadn't bought it from a flim-flam man and arsonist. Are they sure he wasn't the one who put that body in your dumpster?"

"Yeah, it wasn't him. I bought my new soda machine from him too, but the restaurant supply company and the manufacturer are all that matter. He was just the middle man."

"I guess." She set down a perfect cappuccino in front of me with a heart-shape in the froth. "I know you're a standard brew kind of gal, but you have to try one of these."

"It looks delicious."

I heard the door open behind me.

"Here's Joan right now," Julia said.

Joan got her coffee, and I invited her to join me at a table in the corner.

"So, you're working on the weekend, I see," I said to her.

"Oh, yeah. That's the life of a Realtor, Mercy."

I nodded. "And of a restaurant proprietor," I added.

"You're not looking for a new house already, are you?"

"Oh, no, Joan. I love my little house. I just wanted to catch up. I haven't seen you in forever. You know, I was here the other night, and I was wondering if you knew anything about that ballroom dancing class above the barbershop. I saw a lot of people coming and going. My neighbor is new in town, and she's looking for some outlets to meet people."

"Well, Bud and Elena seem to enjoy it. They always stop in before and after to say hello, and they're always in a much better mood afterwards." She smiled and laughed. "Your friend should give it a try. You should too, if you have time. They draw people from Calhoun and Ballers Ferry and as far away as Harro's Bend, so it's not just the local farmers. The distillery expansion has brought in a lot of new blood and younger people too, Mercy."

"That sounds…pretty cool." I was just asking to pry into why the mayor and his wife were in her office the night of the stakeout, but now I'm actually interested in the class. "So, what else is new? Are you going to stop into the town hearing about the street upgrades on the south half of town?"

She leaned across the table and looked at me. "I'm on the council, Mercy! I have to be there."

I slapped my forehead. "I knew that, Joan. I suppose now that Tom is…gone…there won't be much opposition anymore. You have properties over there, don't you? So, you probably are in favor of the project."

"Well, I believe that the street project is something that Paint Creek has needed for a long time, and it's just going to get more expensive every year. But Tom's tragic death doesn't mean that we aren't going to give the opposition a full and fair hearing, Mercy. He had some very good points, and the people deserve to know what it's going to cost, where the money will come from, and what other projects will have to be put on the back burner…"

She sounded very fair and concerned, and I let

her keep talking.

"…but, you know a lot of people are getting hurt by falling property values. Some are having their loans called in because their home value is less than their mortgage balance. People will be losing their houses if this proposal doesn't pass."

"Really? I heard values were down, but I didn't know that there could be foreclosures."

"A lot of people took out second mortgages from the bank at low rates, but now the bank wants its money back. And as far as I'm concerned, I just have one small one-bedroom rental near there, but it's not on a street that will be part of the project. If you see the Realty House logo on yard signs or newspaper ads for rentals, those are Gilbert's. The brothers still own about a dozen properties there, and they still own the rights to the Realty House name for rental management. I own the brand for real estate sales."

"Interesting."

"Well," she looked at her watch, "I have to meet a young couple in the office in a few minutes. I'll stop in for lunch at the diner soon." She got up from her chair and smiled. "Do you still have that hot turkey blue plate special?"

"Every Wednesday!" I said.

"See you Wednesday!"

So far, my day was right on schedule. I called Deloris, and everything was fine at the diner, so I stopped at the grocery store and got a nice fruit basket, picked up my meats at the butcher shop, and then stopped at Ruby's house. I gave her the basket and filled her in on the idea I had for exposing the murderer. This was going to be a good day.

Chapter Fifteen

The town council members were all lined up at
the head table in the second-floor great hall of the
Village Hall. The Mayor, Bud Finster, was in the
middle, and Joan Pianowski was on his right. The
crimson curtain on the stage behind them was
closed, with the official Paint Creek seal
displayed above it. Several dozen folding chairs
were set up facing the council, in the area that was
most often used for dancing or banquet tables for
the town's pancake breakfasts.

There was a podium with a microphone set up
on each side of the long table. They always set up
town hall meetings this way so that the pros and
cons would each have a mic and could debate
each other and ask questions. There was an arc of
eight chairs set up behind the podium on each side
for those of us who wanted to speak. I took a chair
on the "con" side, even though I liked the idea of
improving the streets in the part of town that I
grew up in.

Brody came down the aisle between the
folding chairs for the gallery of observers, which
was almost full. He was looking from side to side
– for me, I hoped. I waved to him and met him by
the front row of chairs.

"Just stopped in to say hello, Mercy. Can't
stay. I thought Bud might need some help finding

the metal detector wand, but it looks like Agent 007 already has things under control."

I smiled and looked at the entry door, where Junior was having the time of his life wanding the people as they came in. "Agent 007?" I asked. "More like *Paul Blart, Mall Cop,* I think."

Brody smiled. "Well, I have to take the state inspectors on a tour of Paint Creek and then through the office and arsenal downstairs here," he said as he looked me up and down. "Did you have to wear a dress?"

I panicked. "What's wrong with it? Do I look frumpy?"

He chuckled. "It's just that I'm a leg man, Mercy, and you've got the best legs in Mclean County."

"I have bony knees."

"Then I guess I like bony knees. Now I'm going to be distracted all day thinking about you – and I might have to stop at your place after dark too."

"Well, Sheriff Hayes, how do you know I'll let you in?"

"I'll bring Häagen-Dazs."

He knows me too well. "Bourbon Praline and

Peppermint Bark."

"Two?" He said, trying to put a convincing look of skepticism on his face.

"Why not?"

"Well – two for you, two for me. I'll have to wake you up in the middle of the night, then."

"You better be there, now," I said, rubbing his chest and arm very briefly. "And by the way, you'd better stop in as soon as you're done with your tour." Then I whispered to him, "And make sure you bring a set of handcuffs."

He gave me a seductive look.

"Not for me! I'll be solving your murder case in the next hour, and you'll have a killer to bring in."

"Really…? Don't get anybody killed, now."

The Mayor gave the gavel a few preliminary bangs, and I said goodbye to Brody. Everybody started moving to their seats. I saw Jake and Junior standing like sergeants at arms on either side of the main entry at the back of the hall – Junior with the wand held up conspicuously in his hand – and I gave them a thumbs-up. Ruby came running in and joined me in front. I gave her an inquiring look, and she gave me two confirming nods. Hattie Harper from the Ladies' Aid Society and Liz Farber from the salon were the only other people on the "Con" side.

I checked my email on my phone, and the photos I asked for from Sylvia were there. Red was sitting on the "Pro" side with most of the whittling club and quite a few others, some of whom had to stand behind the eight chairs set out for them. All the pieces were falling into place.

Just as the mayor gaveled the meeting to order, I saw Tom Hopkins' widow, Patty, come in the door and take a seat in the last row of chairs. She was very pregnant and holding her toddler by the hand.

"Okay, let's get to it," Mayor Bud Finster said. "You all know why we're here. We'll start with a few words from one of the proponents of the street project – Pete Jenkins, you're first in line, you go first – and Hattie on the opposing side. You can ask each other, or any of the council members, questions. Go ahead, Pete."

Pete made his comments about how the new streets would help attract new people to Paint Creek and make things safer for kids on their bicycles. Hattie just really seemed to be there to represent the opposing side to support Tom Hopkins and Patty, but she didn't have much to say.

Ronnie Towns from the hardware store and Liz from the salon went next. It looks like Liz was on Tom's side, so she had no apparent motive to kill him. They talked and argued for nearly 15 minutes and then sat down.

"Okay, thank you," Bud said. "Red and Mercy, you two can go ahead."

I gave Red the evil eye. He knew what his job was over there on the "Pro" side.

"Uh, Bud…er, Mayor," Red said, "I'm still getting my thoughts together. I'm going to yield my time to the next person…Dickie, would you mind going before me?"

Dickie Gallagher got up eagerly. "Sure, Red. I know what I want to say." He stood up, went to the podium, and looked back at his brother, Gilbert, who still had his arm in a sling and seemed to be very pale and suffering in pain. Then Dickie tapped the microphone a few times to make sure it was working. He looked at me, at the podium on the other end of the head table. "Ladies first, Mercy. You go ahead."

"Thanks, Dickie." I paused and looked at the good-sized crowd. There must have been 80 people in the room. "I'm not really sure that I'm opposed to the street proposal, but I've looked at Tom's pamphlet, and I want to make sure that we are taking care of our schools and parks too."

"Well, you don't have to worry about taking money away from the parks and schools, Mercy," Dickie said. "The people with houses on the streets that are being fixed up will be assessed for part of the cost on our property taxes, and the rest is coming from a Federal grant that our Congressman got us for community renewal and infrastructure."

Dickie really seemed to know a lot about it. "But what about our parks and schools, Dickie?" I asked him. "Tom said the money should be spent for those things instead."

Dickie seemed to get a little red in the face and irritated when I mentioned Tom. "The money's not supposed to go for education – that money comes from the state, Mercy. We can pass a school bond if we want new schools too, you know. And Paley Park got all new ball fields and picnic areas with new benches and nice stone grills and a big pavilion with a real nice kitchen. That was just seven or eight years ago. Paint Creek has needed real streets for 50 years – streets with curbs and gutters and storm sewers so we don't get wet basements every time it rains. Eighth Street is still gravel, Mercy."

I wondered why he seemed to dislike Tom – everybody in town always liked him. "That sounds reasonable, Dickie, but why do you think Tom was so opposed to the project then?"

Dickie was getting agitated. He looked over at his brother, Gilbert, and at me. Then he boiled over and banged his fist down on the podium.

"Everybody thinks that Tom Hopkins is a good guy, but he's not!"

There was a gasp from the crowd. I was nervous and hoped this wouldn't get out of hand. I looked at Tom's widow in the back row, and she looked calm.

"You think Tom really wanted to build schools for our kids?" Dickie asked, getting control of himself. "Well, he didn't! He just wanted to keep property values down for one more year so he could steal all of our houses – Gilbert's and mine, and some others too."

Everybody in the gallery began talking, and Bud brought down the gavel.

"We'll have order here. Dickie, we're not here to speak ill of the dead. Keep your comments pertinent to the street issue."

"Let him talk!" Someone yelled for the crowd.

"Yeah. We want to hear him out!"

"I think Tom was trying to take our house

too!"

The gavel came down hard several more times, and the hall became quiet.

"Go ahead, Dickie," Bud said, "but keep it brief."

I wasn't expecting anything like this. I wondered if Dickie was getting senile, or if he really had a reason to be upset with Tom Hopkins. "Dickie," I said to him gently. "What do you mean? How was Tom trying to steal your houses?" Poor Patty had tears streaming down her face now.

"Well, Mercy, you know he started doing all the home loans for the bank a few years ago. So, Gilbert and I were getting ready to retire, and all 14 of our houses were paid for. So, he called us over when we were in the bank one day last year. He said he could give us a loan on each of the houses so we would have money for retirement and money to travel and remodel the house we live in."

I nodded. "I remember you went on that long cruise last year, and Jake and Junior renovated your whole house and added a wrap-around porch while you were away."

"That's right. Well, he set it up so that the payments would come out of our account automatically, and he even added an insurance policy so that everything would be paid in full when either Gilbert or me kicked the bucket. Seemed real sweet for a while. But then six months ago we got a letter in the mail saying he was calling in the loan. We had 30 days to pay it in full, or he was going to take all of our houses."

"But why was he calling in the loan, Dickie? How can he do that? And didn't you have most of the money still in the bank to pay it?" Something didn't seem right here.

"Good questions. It seems Tom put a little clause in our loan that said if our property value fell below a certain percentage of our loan balance, he could cancel the loan and make us pay it in full right away. Well, somebody got the county assessor to cut the value of our houses in half because they were on 'unimproved streets.' And we couldn't pay it back because all of the money in our bank account mysteriously got transferred to a bank in the Cayman Islands – and there was no way we could prove the account there wasn't ours. A little while later, Tom started building that new mansion over northeast. Can I keep talking, mayor?"

Everyone wanted to hear more, and Bud just nodded.

"So, all of our houses are in foreclosure now.

But if the new streets are approved now and the funding for the project is guaranteed by the government, I could appeal the assessed value and save our properties. But as it is, the bank will get them, and Tom is set to become president of the bank next month. He was going to buy all our houses from the bank for pennies on the dollar – with my money, the money he stole from me and Gilbert. Then, when he lets the street bill go through a year from now, they will all be worth ten times what he pays for them."

The crowd couldn't hold back any longer, and they sounded like a den of hungry lions.

Sandy Skitter stood up. "He was doing the same thing to me," she said. "I just never realized until now that it was all an evil plan."

There were shouts of "Me too!"

"Dickie," I said into my microphone three times, and the crowd gradually quieted down again, with a little help from Bud's gavel.

"Yes, ma'am?" He was emotional and on the verge of tears.

I looked at him and asked as gently as I could, "Is that why you killed him, Dickie?"

The crowd went into an uproar again, and Bud gaveled it down.

"Miss Howard," the Mayor said, "you can't just go slinging accusations like that around in a public forum."

"But I have the proof, Mayor. It's true, isn't it, Dickie?"

"I ain't saying nothing."

"Well, sawdust, which we can prove came from your whittling knife, was found on Tom's shirt collar." I held up my phone and Ruby's too. "And the marks on his body match the pattern from the floor mat in your trunk."

He snapped his head toward me. "Nobody's looked in my trunk, Mercy, so you're lying."

"It's the truth, Dickie. When Ruby stopped by with that fruit basket this morning, I followed her over there and let the air out of one of her tires, and she left her jack at home. So, when you changed the tire for her, you had to use your own jack, and she snapped these pictures inside your trunk when you opened it. It looks like Tom's silk necktie is still in there too – that's the murder weapon, right?"

Dickie looked like a cornered rat with nowhere to run. He was sweating profusely now, and he ran behind the head table, but the Mayor stood up to stop him. He was no match for Dickie.

Dickie put his strong arm around Bud's neck, holding him like a hostage in front of him, and pulled out his pocket knife. "You all leave me alone and let me out of here, or I swear I'll cut his throat!"

Great...now I caused a hostage situation, and Brody isn't back yet. "Dickie," I said. "You don't have to do this."

"I didn't mean to kill anybody, Mercy..."

Just then the curtain opened slightly on the stage behind Dickie and Bud, and the barrel of a handgun stuck it's nose out. Then we all heard the sound of the gun being cocked.

Chapter Sixteen

"Don't turn around, Dickie," Deloris said, stepping out in front of the curtain.

"How did you get in here with a gun, Deloris?" Dickie asked. "We all had to go through a metal detector today."

"That was easy, Dickie. I told them I had a steel plate in my head. My Remington six-shooter fits nicely in my beehive."

"You're not going to shoot me in the back. At this distance, the bullet would go right through me and kill Bud too."

"Well, I never cared that much for Bud, anyway. He can be kind of a pompous ass. No big loss."

There were chuckles from the crowd, although Bud didn't seem to see the humor in it.

"But I do like you, Dickie. Always have. You always protected the girls, carried our books...

"But none of the girls ever like me...because I was different."

"I liked you, Dickie. Do you remember that time when you carried me across that big puddle in the street after a big rainfall? I was in high school and you were still in junior high."

"Yes."

"Do you remember what I did afterwards?"

Dickie paused and then nodded. "Yes."

"What did I do?"

He looked around, but didn't speak.

"Go ahead, Dickie," Deloris said very calmly. "Tell them."

"You let me touch your face."

There was a low rumble and some laughter from the crowd.

"That's right. And you liked that, didn't you, Dickie? I liked it to. It's too bad that people back then didn't understand autism and Asperger's."

"They still don't! People treat me like I'm stupid or a child! But I'm not!"

"No, you're not. I think you showed everyone here today just how smart you really are, Dickie." Deloris sat down on the front edge of the stage. She had held the gun down a long time ago, but we were all to enthralled in the conversation to notice.

"But I'm 'socially awkward.' That's why I could never have a girl or a family." He was trying very hard to hold back his emotions.

"Dickie," Deloris said gently, "now I want you to tell me what happened the night that Tom was killed. Tell us all how Tom ended up dead in Mercy's dumpster."

"You can't trick me, Deloris." He still had his back to her, but he was hardly holding onto Bud at all and his pocket knife was at his side. "Nothing I say will stand up in court because you're holding a gun on me."

"Perfect. I don't want you to get in trouble with the law anyway. So, tell us."

Bud reached down to the table in front of him, grabbed his microphone and held it up for Dickie.

"Well, Tom knew that we were going to tell our story to everybody at the next council meeting, so he got it changed from Thursday to Tuesday, and nobody told us. We figured that if we exposed what Tom was doing, that the council would vote for the new streets and we would be able to keep our properties.

"Then, when we were finishing up our whittling meeting the same night as the council meeting, about nine o'clock or so, I guess, Tom called Gilbert on his phone. He said that the vote failed – which wasn't true; it just got delayed – and he wanted to meet us right away. He said he had an idea to help us that would save our properties. Well, you know that little sitting area with tables out in back of our old real estate office downtown. It's Joan Pianowski's office now. The agents use it for lunch or smoking or talking to clients sometimes, and he wanted to meet us there. But he didn't bring us there to help us…he brought us there to kill us."

What! Is this possible? Can this meeting possibly get any stranger!

"Tell us what happened, Dickie," Deloris said casually, leaning back on her arms now, as Bud gaveled down the crowd again.

"Okay. We pulled up and Tom was standing by one of the tables in the corner. When we got close, we saw that he had a gun and big smile on his face. We asked what he was doing, and he said that since the houses were collateral on the loan, and the loan was in default now, that he was now the beneficiary on the insurance he sold us. That's how he set it up. So, if one of us died he would get all the insurance money. And pretty soon he would own the houses too. He asked which one of us wanted to die first, and Gilbert said he did. Gilbert said he should just kill him and leave me alone, because only one of us had to die for him to collect the insurance."

Gilbert was in tears now too, and Dickie was barely in control of himself.

"I walked towards Tom and said, 'You're not going to kill Gilbert.' And he said 'No – you are!' He said he was going to make it look like we were really sad about losing everything and got into a fight. People would say that I killed Gilbert and then killed myself. They would believe that, he said, because the whole town thinks I'm crazy. He figured our old office would be a good place to stage the murders. Then he started laughing, and I ran towards him. He raised his gun and fired just as I dove at him. I pushed his gun hand, and the bullet hit Gilbert in the shoulder."

Wow! There was a gasp from the crowd again, and Bud pounded his gavel. *I guess that would explain why his arm has been in a sling since that day.*

Deloris continued to moderate the conversation. "What happened next, Dickie?"

"He fell to the ground, and the gun slid away. I held his shoulders down, and I was really mad. He shot my brother, and it was my fault, because he was trying to shoot me, and I pushed his hand."

"But you didn't hit him." I said, finally speaking again. "There were no bruises on his face."

"Gilbert told me not to hurt him, Mercy. I pulled him up by his necktie, and Gilbert picked up the gun and threw it in the little dumpster. He didn't want Patty to find out about any of this, so we decided not to tell anybody."

"What happened then?" Deloris asked him. "Why did you kill him?"

Dickie got really red in the face, pushed Bud away, and then turned around toward Deloris. "He called me a dummy! He said I was a big dumb oaf, so I grabbed him the way I was holding Bud just now, and my hand was shaking…and I put my pocket knife up to his neck. Gilbert hollered at me to stop, so I pulled my knife away. But it's really sharp and I cut him a little bit. Then I pushed him away. He stood there and took off his necktie. He was going to wipe the blood off his neck with his handkerchief, but first he laughed at me and called me a big dummy again. Everything went red, and I guess I grabbed his necktie."

He paused. Bud pulled his chair behind Dickie, and he slumped down into it.

"Next thing I remember, Gilbert is shaking me, and Tom is dead."

Everyone got to their feet, and there wasn't a dry eye in the hall…except for Deloris. She held out her hand to Dickie, and he stood up. I thought she was actually going to show a little compassion and give him a hug. Instead she patted him on the shoulder. "We all understand, Dickie."

Patty Hopkins arrived at the front of the hall.

"I'm really sorry, Patty. We never wanted you to find out about the loans and Tom trying to kill us," Dickie said.

She had to stand on her tiptoes and reach very high to give Dickie a hug. "I knew something was very wrong, Dickie. I just didn't know how bad it really was. I'm so, so sorry."

He bent over and hugged her pregnant body very gently as she kissed him on the cheek.

"And don't worry, Patty," he said. "We're not going to try to take that new house away from you and your kids."

She smiled bravely. "Tom's insurance will take care of us. You'll get everything back, Dickie."

Brody walked in with Deputy Doggerty just then. Stan was holding a plastic bag with a hand gun in it. I had filled Brody in by phone about what was going on. The dumpster at the Realty House had not been emptied yet, and the gun was still there. Dickie's story was true. Brody joined me in the front of the hall.

"Nobody got shot," I said to him.

"I don't think you get extra points for that. You know I have to cuff him, right?"

I sighed and nodded. We walked over to Dickie, and Deloris took the cuffs from Brody.

"Sorry, Dickie," she told him, "but you know the way this is done."

He nodded glumly and turned around with his wrists together behind him.

"The whole meeting was recorded, you know, just like all the town meetings," Deloris said, "so, I think things are going to turn out okay for you."

"Time to go, Mr. Gallagher," Brody said with a smile as he passed Dickie off to his deputy.

"Dickie…" I said before they took him away, "…just one more thing: Why did you put Tom in my dumpster? There was a dumpster right there at the real estate office where all of this happened."

He nodded and slowly looked me in the eye. "Well, they pick up the garbage at Realty House on Mondays, and this happened on Tuesday night. We knew that they come to your place on Wednesday because when we get done eating breakfast we always go into the kitchen to talk to Smoke. We always hear the garbage truck out there when we're tasting the turkey that Smoke roasted for the Wednesday special. He always gives us a slice. So, we thought that the body would be gone fast. We didn't know somebody was going to set it on fire. I'm really sorry about that."

I felt badly for Dickie as Stan took him out of the hall. I was just like everybody else, thinking that Dickie wasn't very bright, but he's really brilliant. I was amazed at how well he understood and explained all of the banking and politics that were going on. He figured out Tom's complicated scheme all by himself.

I took Brody's hand. "One year in a nice, low security psych ward where they'll help him find some self-esteem – max! I'll find a nice woman for him."

"I'll see what I can do, counselor."

Ruby and Deloris and the others were still in a circle talking about the remarkable revelations. I waved to them as Brody and I headed for the exit. It seemed like most everybody in the hall wanted to stay and talk for a while. Nobody was leaving.

He put his arm around my shoulders. "Say, Mercy…how about if we pick up that ice cream and stop by your place right now?"

"I'm not in the mood for ice cream." I took his

hand as we walked toward the exit. "Besides, half of these people will be heading for the diner pretty soon. Deloris and Babs will need help."

He seemed disappointed. "But, by the time they all get done chatting here and all the orders get put in to the kitchen and cooked up, they won't really need help for at least an hour."

I looked around at the crowd and considered his wisdom. Then I began walking briskly, pulling Brody along. "So, we'd better hurry! Last one to the car is a rotten egg!"

"We'll take my car...I've got lights and sirens!"

Smoke's Hungarian Chops based on my Grandmother, Lorene Forgey's, recipe:

Ingredients:

4 pork chops
3 tablespoons oil
Paprika
Diced onion
2 cups button mushrooms
Salt and pepper
Bay leaf
1 cup chicken broth
1 tablespoon cornstarch
2 tablespoons water

1 cup sour cream (optional)
Caraway seeds (optional)

Cover both sides of the chops with a generous amount
of paprika. Heat the oil in a large skillet and place the
chops in the pan when oil is hot. Brown the chops on
both sides. Add caraway seeds on top of the chops while
cooking. Remove the chops from the pan after
browning. Add diced onion and button mushrooms.
Saute for 2 minutes. Place the chops back into the skillet
along with a bay leaf and 1 cup chicken broth. Cover
and cook on low for one hour. Mix a tablespoon of
cornstarch with 2 tablespoons of water. Remove the
chops from the skillet and add the cornstarch mixture.
Increase the heat until mixture is boiling, stirring
constantly. Return the chops to the gravy after it has
thickened. You may also add 1 cup of sour cream to the
gravy. Serve over mashed potatoes or noodles.

Lorene Forgey's Baked Apples Ala Mode

6 cooking apples
1 cup brown sugar
1 cup water
2 tablespoons butter

Wash, core and pare the apples ½ of the way down the
apple from the top. Place apples in a baking dish.
Prepare the syrup by cooking the brown sugar, water
and butter in a sauce pan over low heat. When the

mixture becomes syrupy, pour it over the apples. Bake the apples at 350 degrees for 45 to 55 minutes depending on the size of the apples. Serve apples slightly warm with ice cream.

Thanks for reading! I hope you enjoyed the book and it would mean so much to me if you could leave a review. Reviews help authors gain more exposure and keep us writing your favorite stories.

You can find all of my books by visiting my Author Page.

Sign up for Constance Barker's New Releases Newsletter where you can find out when my next book is coming out and for special discounted pricing.

I never share or sell your email.

Visit me on Facebook and give me feedback on the characters and their stories.

The We're Not Dead Yet Club

Fetch a Pail of Murder

Wedding Bells and Death Knells

Murder or Bust

Pinched, Pilfered and a Pitchfork

A Hot Spot of Murder

Witchy Women of Coven Grove Series

The Witching on the Wall

A Witching Well of Magic

Witching the Night Away

Witching There's Another Way

Witching Your Life Away

Witching You Wouldn't Go

Witching for a Miracle

Teasen & Pleasen Hair Salon Series

A Hair Raising Blowout

Wash, Rinse, Die

Holiday Hooligans

Color Me Dead

False Nails & Tall Tales

Caesar's Creek Series

A Frozen Scoop of Murder (Caesars Creek Mystery Series Book One)

Death by Chocolate Sundae (Caesars Creek Mystery Series Book Two)

Soft Serve Secrets (Caesars Creek Mystery Series Book Three)

Ice Cream You Scream (Caesars Creek Mystery Series Book Four)

Double Dip Dilemma (Caesars Creek Mystery Series Book Five)

Melted Memories (Caesars Creek Mystery Series Book Six)

Triple Dip Debacle(Caesars Creek Mystery Series Book Seven)

Whipped Wedding Woes(Caesars Creek Mystery Series Book Eight)

A Sprinkle of Tropical Trouble(Caesars Creek Mystery Series Book Nine)

A Drizzle of Deception(Caesars Creek Mystery Series

Book Ten)

Sweet Home Mystery Series

Whispering Pines Mystery Series

Curse of the Bloodstone Arrow (Whispering Pines Mystery Series)

Fright Night at the Haunted Inn (Whispering Pines Mystery Series)

Mad River Mystery Series

A Wicked Whack

A Prickly Predicament

A Malevolent Menace

Made in the USA
Monee, IL
08 November 2024

69667698R00090